Paul Bowles was born in Ne 1931 to study music with Aar Jane Auer, herself a gifted n to achieve literary fame. Afte which is now Bowles' perm first novel, *The Sheltering Sky* hit at the cinema, he has a acclaimed novels – *Let It Come Down, The Spider's House* and *Up Above the World* – all of which confirm his reputation as a writer of exceptional talent and distinction.

By the same author

Fiction

Pages From Cold Point
The Sheltering Sky
Let It Come Down
The Spider's House
Up Above the World

(With Mohammed Mrabet)
The Lemon
Love with a Few Hairs

Non-Fiction

Points in Time
Their Heads Are Green
Without Stopping

PAUL BOWLES

Midnight Mass

and other stories

Paladin
An Imprint of HarperCollinsPublishers

Paladin
An Imprint of HarperCollins*Publishers*
77–85 Fulham Palace Road,
Hammersmith, London W6 8JB

Published by Paladin 1991
1 3 5 7 9 8 6 4 2

First British Commonwealth edition
published by Peter Owen Ltd 1985

ISBN 0 586 09206 4

Printed in Great Britain by
HarperCollinsManufacturing Glasgow

Contents

Midnight Mass

He arrived in Tangier at noon and went straight to the house. In the rain the outer courtyard was uninviting. Several dead banana plants had fallen over and been left to rot on the tile floor. Even as old Amina, seeing him from the kitchen doorway, waddled out into the rain to greet him, he was aware of the piles of empty crates, and of the frame of an ancient garden swing looming behind her.

At lunch he tasted his childhood in Amina's soup. The recipe had not changed; pumpkin and cumin still predominated. All at once he was aware of a cold wind blowing through the room. He called to Amina: the big window in the kitchen was broken. He reminded her that money had been sent to have it repaired. But the wind had come and blown it in again, she said, and this time they had simply left it that way. He told her to shut the door to the kitchen. When she had done it he could not see that it made any difference.

He went through the rooms. The place was only a shell of the house he remembered. Most of the furniture was gone, and there were no rugs or curtains. When he discovered that all six of the fireplaces belched smoke, he had his first doubts about the usefulness of the house as a place to spend the Christmas holidays – at least, that year. It was the only bequest his mother had made him, and she had been reluctant even about that. 'You don't want the house in Tangier. You'll never use it.' 'But I love it,' he objected. 'I grew up in it, after all.' Once she had agreed to leave it to him, she had proceeded to strip it of everything of value. A rug went to one friend, a highboy to another, a chest to someone else, so that by the time she died, the house must have been in more or less its present state. Several times during the eight years since her death his wife had urged him to go and 'take stock' of the house, but since her interest was based on the possibility of selling it, a thing he intended never to do, he had taken no action.

The house was in even worse condition than he had expected it to be. Ingenuously, he had assumed that because he paid their wages promptly each month, the servants would make an attempt to keep it in order. He hoped for some hot water to get the chimney soot off his hands, but Mohammed told him that the water heater had not functioned since the year before Madame had died. The man she called in to repair it had said it would have to be replaced by a new system, so she had used cold water after that. As he dried his hands on a flimsy linen guest-towel (she had given away all the bathtowels) he thought grimly: She could let old Madame Schreiber go off with a rug worth several thousand pounds, but she couldn't afford to bathe in hot water.

He went out into the garden. The rain had stopped, but the wind moved the trees, so that large scattered drops still fell as they swayed. He looked up at the huge white façade, marvelling that he ever could have thought it majestic. Now it looked like a pavilion left over from a long-forgotten exposition.

By the end of the afternoon he was thoroughly chilled. The house was too close to the sea. The wind came up over the cliff laden with the salt mist of the waves, and sprayed it against the windows. If he looked out at the garden he saw it only confusedly through the curtain of salt that had coated the panes. In the library closet he found an electric heater. It was ancient, but it gave off a modest glow. With the shutters bolted and the door closed, he seized a book at random from the bookshelves and threw himself into a chair. He read for a moment, then turned to the back of the book and on a blank page began to compose a telegram to his wife. CANCEL FLIGHT HOUSE DISASTROUS REPAIRS IMPERATIVE RETURNING FIRST

WEEK JANUARY ALAS NO CHRISTMAS TOGETHER PLAN FOR
EASTER HERE BETTER SEASON ALL LOVE. Early spring could
be very cold, too, he suddenly remembered, but at least the fireplaces would be working.

He had instructed his Tangier bank to have the telephone
connected; it was an agreeable surprise to hear the operator's
voice. The difficulties began as he tried to spell out the name
and address. '*M comme en Marseille? R comme en Robert?*' There
was an explosion of clicks, and the connection faded. He hung
up and dialled the taxi service. The cab waited for him outside
the post-office.

The first few nights he slept badly. The sheets were damp
and there were not enough blankets. Even with the windows
shut the sea wind raced through the big bedroom. Each
morning well before dawn a pair of owls settled in the cypress
trees beside the house and began to call back and forth. In his
childhood he had heard the sound many times, but it never had
kept him awake.

When the wind had turned and the days grew sunny, the
workmen were able to start rebuilding the chimneys. The
house was full of Moroccans in overalls and rubber boots. It
was Ramadan; they worked without speaking, feeling their
hunger and thirst in silence.

On the Sunday before Christmas the sky was bright blue
and cloudless. The north wind had brought the mountains in
Spain unusually near. Since no workmen would be coming, he
decided to go out for a walk. The puddles in the road had dried.
Plant odours and the scent of woodsmoke laced the wind. In a
better mood, he conceived the idea of asking a few people to
come by on Christmas Eve for drinks; it would be pleasanter
than having to go out, and he could not envisage remaining
alone in the house on that night.

A small white car came into view and drew up outside an
iron-grilled gate a hundred feet or so ahead of him. As he
approached, he recognized Madame Dervaux. As soon
as they had greeted one another, he mentioned Christmas Eve,
suggesting that she bring along anyone she wished. She

accepted immediately; she would try, she said, to be with interesting people. He was about to make a facetious reply, but seeing that she was perfectly serious, he held his tongue.

During the next few days he invited a few more people. Although he did not much care who came, since he only wanted to see someone in the house on Christmas Eve, he reflected with satisfaction that not one of the prospective guests would have been asked to the house by his mother.

Christmas Eve was clear and almost windless. The moon, directly overhead, filled the courtyard with its hard light. Amina had just carried the last tray of glasses into the hall when the doctor arrived. Once he was seated, a gin and tonic in his hand, he looked around the room and frowned.

'Your mother had a great deal to put up with here in this house,' he said. 'It was far too damp for her to live in, and far too big for her to manage.'

He heard the sharpness in his voice as he replied. 'It was her own choice to go on living here. She loved it. She wouldn't have agreed to live anywhere else.'

The rector came in, out of breath and smiling. This was his first winter in Morocco, so the doctor described the climate to him.

Leaving the two talking, he went into the library and lighted the fire Mohammed had laid in the fireplace there. Then he had Amina bring more candles and set them around the room, knowing that the library was where the guests eventually would gather. The other rooms had very little furniture in them.

The sound of laughter came from the courtyard. Madame Dervaux entered, with several younger people in her wake. Going straight up to her host, she presented him with a huge bunch of narcissus. 'Smell,' she told him. 'I picked them this afternoon at Sidi Yamani. The fields are covered.'

He hurried to the kitchen to have Amina put the flowers into water. Madame Dervaux followed, talking rapidly. She had come, she said, with a poet, a painter and a philosopher, all of them Moroccans. As an afterthought she added: 'And a very charming Indian girl from Paris. So you see?'

Understanding this as a reference to her promise to bring 'interesting' people, he set his jaw. Finally he murmured: 'Aha.'

When they returned to the salon, Vandeventer stood in the middle of the room, slightly the worse for having just come from another party. The rector had gone with the younger people into the library. Madame Dervaux, hearing their laughter, walked quickly in their direction.

He settled Vandeventer near the doctor, poured himself a neat Scotch, and wandered in the direction of the library. As he got to the doorway, the rector was saying playfully to one of the young Moroccans: 'You'd better be careful. One of these mornings you may wake up and find yourself in Hell.'

'No, no,' the young man said easily. 'Hell is only for people who haven't suffered enough here.' The rector seemed taken aback.

Fearful that the conversation might be about to degenerate into a quasi-religious discussion among his guests, he went quickly toward the group. 'And you,' he said, singling out the Moroccan, 'you've suffered enough?'

'Too much,' he said simply.

Madame Dervaux rose to her feet and asked to be taken on a tour of inspection of the house. He protested that there was nothing to see but empty rooms.

'But we can see the rooms! And go up into the tower, and out onto the roof. The view is superb.'

'In the dark?'

'In the moonlight, in the moonlight,' she said rapturously. The Moroccans murmured with approval.

'Come,' he told them, and they all followed him out. A young Frenchman and his wife, both of whom taught at the Lycée Regnault, had arrived, bringing with them another couple from Casablanca. He had to leave his little party of sightseers at the foot of the stairs while he saw to it that the new arrivals were supplied with drinks. He poured himself another glass of whisky to take with him on the tour.

Some of the electric bulbs along the way failed to come on, so that there was more darkness than light on the stairways. Even before they got to the tower door they could hear the roar of the sea below.

He went ahead and opened one of the windows, so they could lean out and see the black cliffs of the coastline. The only lights in the landscape were a few twinkling points across the strait in Spain. 'The end of the world,' the rector remarked as he drew in his head.

A moment later when they were back in the hallway, the young Moroccan with whom he had spoken in the library came up from behind and walked along beside him. 'Letting me look at all these empty rooms is very bad,' he said. 'Like showing food to a starving man.'

'How is that?' he asked absently.

'It's only that I have to live with my family, and there's no space anywhere, so what I want most is a room. Nearly every night I dream that I have a room of my own where I can paint. So of course when I see so many rooms with no one in them, the saliva runs in my mouth. It's natural.'

'I suppose it is.' He found the young man's confidences embarrassing; they emphasized the disparities between them, and gave him a vague sense of guilt.

Now Madame Dervaux was clamouring to be taken out onto the roof. He refused. 'There's no railing.'

'We'll just stand in the moonlight,' she insisted. 'No one will go near the edge.'

He stopped walking and stared at her. 'That's exact, since no one is going onto the roof.'

She pouted for an instant, and then resumed her chatter.

On the way downstairs he turned to the painter, who was still beside him. 'I ought to spend more time here,' he said, a note of apology in his voice. 'But the truth is, the house isn't very livable.'

'How can you say that? It's a magnificent house.'

'The wind blows straight through it,' he went on, as though the other had not spoken. 'There are rats in the walls, there's no hot water, half the time the telephone doesn't function.'

'But all houses here are like that. The difference is that this one has ten times as much space.'

So far he had pretended not to see where the painter was attempting to direct the conversation, but now he said: 'I'd like nothing better than to be able to slice off a room for you and wrap it up, so you could take it home.'

The Moroccan smiled. 'Why does it have to be taken home? It could be consumed on the premises just as well.'

He laughed, liking the Moroccan's appropriation of his metaphor. 'Ah yes, there's that too,' he agreed as they arrived back at the library door. 'Just pass by the bar,' he said to those behind him. 'Mohammed will give you what you want.'

Beyond the library was a farther room, forming a separate wing of the house. In bygone days it had been referred to as the conservatory. Now there was nothing in it, and the door into it was kept shut because the many windows let in the sea wind. When he returned from the bar presently, he caught sight of Madame Dervaux striking a theatrical pose as she flung open the door.

'*Mon dieu!*' she cried. 'So *this* is where the corpses are buried!'

Now the library was crowded, so that he was unable to get to the door before she had led both the painter and poet into the dark room. He leaned in and called to them. 'There's no light in there, and we can't have the door open. Please come back.' When they failed to answer, he shut the door.

He heard Madame Dervaux's squeal, waited, then opened the door a crack and held it, so they could find their way back.

Madame Dervaux came out laughing, although she shot a resentful glance at him. The poet continued imperturbably to criticize Baudelaire, but the painter was not listening. 'What a studio!' he murmured.

'It was terrifying, that horrible place, without a ray of light!' Madame Dervaux confided to the Indian girl.

She was insufferable. 'But Madame,' he said. 'Corpses are generally enjoyed in the dark.'

'A fantastic studio,' the painter went on. 'North light, nothing but trees and the sea. A paradise!'

He faced the young man. 'The ceiling is in shreds. The rain has come in everywhere. I doubt one could use it for anything.'

The doctor and the rector were leaving, and the two French couples were conferring on the shortest route to the site of the next party. Vandeventer, leaning against the wall for support, was arguing with the Indian girl. There was a general consulting of timepieces. 'If we're going to Midnight Mass we must leave now,' Madame Dervaux declared.

Vandeventer had begun to walk slowly toward the group. 'Have you ever heard such nonsense?' he demanded of his host, indicating the others with his glass. 'Three Moslems, one Hindu and one atheist, all running off to Midnight Mass? Ridiculous, no?'

He shrugged. 'Ah, well, *de gustibus.* You know.' To himself he said fervently: 'Thank God for Midnight Mass.' Without it they would have stayed indefinitely. The workmen were coming in the morning, the same as on other days, the holiday not being one of theirs.

Vandeventer seized his arm. 'I must leave you. Delightful evening. Already I'm drunk, and now I must take my wife to the reveillon at the Minzah.'

He walked with him to the gate, to prevent him from stumbling in the courtyard. Once Vandeventer had managed to get into the car, he had no difficulty in driving it.

And now the remainder of his guests came filing out. The two French couples said good-night, and Mohammed shut the gate after them. As she slowly led her little group across the open space, Madame Dervaux suddenly announced that they must all take a quick glance at the kitchen, which she qualified as 'superb'. The others followed her, all but the painter, who lagged behind and walked over to his host.

'I hope you enjoy the service,' his host told him.

'Oh, I'm not going with them. I live near here.'

The wind had risen somewhat. He heard Madame Dervaux's shrill expletives and Amina's easy laughter. He stared at the painter. 'Good. Stay a minute after they've gone. I'd like to talk to you.' His mind was made up. 'What difference does it make?' he thought. 'Let him use the room. No one else is ever going to use it.'

The young man nodded, his face taking on an air of secrecy. When the others went out through the gate he said nothing. Instead of getting into the car with Madame Dervaux, he slammed the door shut and waved.

Immediately her head emerged. '*Oh, le méchant!*' she scolded. '*Il va avoir une gueule de bois affreuse!*'

The painter smiled and waved again.

He watched the scene standing in the open gateway. When the tail lights had disappeared up the dark road, he turned to the young man and said: 'I simply wanted to say that I see no objection to letting you use the conservatory.'

The young man's eyes glowed; he expressed his gratitude at some length. When they had shaken hands and he had gone out through the gate, he looked back and said: 'Tonight I won't have to dream of having a room to paint in.'

His host smiled fleetingly and bolted the door. The wind whipped around the banana plants, slapping their leaves one against the other. He was pleased with his decision. The house seemed more real now that he knew someone would be using even that small part of it. He went from room to room, blowing out the candles and switching off the lights. Then he went upstairs to bed. Amina had set a bowl of Madame Dervaux's narcissus on the night table. Their scent reached him, borne on the sea air, as he fell into sleep.

He did not go to Tangier at Easter time, nor yet during the summer. In September he got word that the painter's very rich and influential family had taken possession of the entire house. His lawyer was unable to evict them. Just before Christmas he received notice that the property, having been certified as agricultural land, no longer belonged to him. He reacted quietly to the loss, but his calm was shattered when, a few months later, he learned that the top floor and the tower had been rented by Madame Dervaux.

The Little House

The little house had been built sixty or seventy years ago on the main street of what had been a village several miles outside the town; now the town had crept up on all sides. Originally there had been only the ground floor, but at some point an extra room had been added above the kitchen. In clear weather from one window of the upstairs room it was still possible to see the line of distant mountains to the southwest. It was here that Lalla Aïcha liked to sit, running her fingers over the beads of her chaplet while she considered how greatly her life had changed since her son had brought her to the town to stay with him. Somewhere behind the mountains was the valley where she had passed her life. She did not expect to see it again.

At first she had felt that moving to the town was a great triumph for her, but now she was not certain. It was true that the food was better, and there was plenty of it, but the house was very small, and she felt cramped living in it. Privately she was sorry that Sadek had not found a better wife than Fatoma, even though Fatoma's parents owned a large house not far away. It seemed to her that in return for having married their useless daughter, Sadek might have been offered a part of their house to live in. They all could have lived there easily, without getting in each other's way. But when she mentioned it to Sadek, he merely laughed.

The young people had been married for more than a year, and there was no sign of a child, a circumstance which Lalla Aïcha blamed on the girl, unaware that the couple had agreed to

16

start a family only when they had some money set aside for the purpose.

As for Fatoma, she had been nervous and unhappy since the day Lalla Aïcha had moved in with them. The old woman was particular about her food, and found constant fault with Fatoma's method of keeping house. Whatever the girl happened to be doing, Lalla Aïcha would stand watching her closely, then shake her head and say: That's not the way we did it in my day, when Moulay Youssef was alive. She felt that Fatoma was too casual about serving Sadek's dinner to him when he came in from work.

Why should he have to wait half an hour before he can eat? she demanded. Why don't you have everything ready so you can bring in the taifor as soon as you hear him come in? He's too good to you, that's the trouble, and you take advantage of his easy nature.

Then Lalla Aïcha would get Sadek aside and tell him how much Fatoma disliked her and how insultingly she treated her. She won't take me out for a walk, and she won't let me go to market with her. I like to get out once in a while, but I can't go by myself. And the other day when she took me to the doctor's, she went so fast I couldn't catch my breath. I know, she wishes I were dead, that's all.

Sadek laughed and said: You're crazy.

Ever since the older woman had moved in with them, Fatoma had been trying to persuade her to discard her haïk and wear a djellaba like other women of the town, but Lalla Aïcha disapproved strongly of djellabas on women, saying that Moulay Youssef would surely have forbidden such a shameless custom. For Fatoma the haïk was an emblem of rusticity; above all she did not want to be taken for a girl from the country. It filled her with shame to walk in the street beside a tottering old woman in a haïk.

Each time she could slip it into the conversation, Fatoma reminded Lalla Aïcha that she had been given the best room in the house. They both knew this was not the case. True, it had more windows and better light than the room where the married couple slept. But it was upstairs, and with each heavy rain the roof sprang new leaks, while Sadek and Fatoma were snug in a room near the kitchen.

Neither of them was sure enough of her position in the household to risk a show of open hostility; each had the fear that Sadek might unaccountably side with the other. Thus they were quiet in his presence, and life in the house continued with relative tranquillity.

For a long time Lalla Aïcha had been aware that a fleshy growth was developing in the middle of her spine, although she had mentioned it to no one. One day as he helped her rise from the floor where she had been sitting, Sadek felt the bulbous object beneath her clothing, and cried out in surprise. It was not an easy matter to persuade her to see a doctor, but Sadek was determined, and eventually had his way. The doctor advised prompt removal of the tumour, and set a date for the operation.

During the days immediately prior to her hospitalization the old woman fretted. She had heard that the anaesthetic was something to be dreaded, she was afraid she might bleed to death, and she made it very clear that she had no faith in Nazarene medicines.

It's all right, Sadek told her. You're going to be fine.

The night before she was to leave, Sadek and Fatoma sat in their room discussing the probable cost of the operation. Lalla Aïcha had gone upstairs and was getting her things together to be packed.

All the money I've saved trying to make cheap meals, Fatoma said with bitterness.

If it were your own mother you wouldn't feel that way, he told her.

She did not answer. There was a knock at the door. Lalla Halima, an elderly woman who lived across the street, had come to call on Lalla Aïcha and bid her good-bye.

She's upstairs, said Fatoma listlessly. Sighing and groaning, the woman mounted the staircase, and Sadek and Fatoma continued their unhappy discussion.

In the morning after Lalla Aïcha had gone to the hospital, and Sadek and Fatoma were having breakfast, Sadek looked around the room. It seems different, having her gone, doesn't it?

It's quiet, said Fatoma.

He turned quickly to her. I know you don't like having her here. I know she makes you nervous. But she's my mother.

Fatoma assumed an injured air. I only said it was quiet, and it is.

That afternoon when Sadek came home from work, Fatoma handed him a large basket. He lifted it. It's heavy, he said.

Take it to your mother in the hospital. It's a tajine with lemon, still hot.

It was his mother's favourite dish. By Allah, she's going to be very happy! he said, and he kissed Fatoma, happy that she should have gone to such trouble.

When he got to the hospital the doors were locked. He tapped on the glass. A guard came who told him that visiting hours were over, and that in any case no food from outside could be taken in. Sadek cajoled, pleaded, threatened, but it had no result. The guard shut the door, leaving him on the steps with the basket.

Both he and Fatoma heartily disliked tajine with lemon, so that he saw no purpose in carrying it back home. It would be a sin to waste it; someone must eat it while it was hot. Then he thought of Fatoma's parents, who lived just down the street from the hospital. They liked the old-fashioned dishes, and would surely appreciate being brought a fresh tajine.

He found Fatoma's mother in the kitchen, greeted her, and took the pot out of the basket. Here's a tajine Fatoma just made, he told her.

She burst into smiles. Si Mohammed's going to be very happy when he sees what we're going to eat tonight, she said.

Early the following morning, before Sadek had eaten his breakfast, there was a great banging on the door. The two police officers who stood outside seized him and without allowing him to say good-bye to Fatoma, forced him into a jeep.

His mystification did not last long. At the comisaría they confronted him with the basket and the pot, which still had a good amount of the tajine in it. He was made to understand that the food was full of poison, and that his mother-in-law was dead. Si Mohammed, who lay in the hospital, had accused him of her murder.

At that point only one thought occupied Sadek's mind: Fatoma had tried to kill his mother. Confused by the lengthy questioning, he muttered aloud some of his inward preoccupations; these scraps caught the attention of the police.

Allah has punished her! She meant to kill mine, and she killed her own.

They soon learned that he was talking about his wife, but placed no credence in his account until the hospital guard had been called in and had verified it. The man remembered Sadek very distinctly, he said, because he had been so annoyingly insistent upon getting the food delivered to his mother.

They sent for Fatoma. She was overcome by the news of her mother's death, and stunned by Sadek's sudden arrest. Her replies were inarticulate beyond her admission that she had given Sadek the basket with the pot of tajine in it, and told him to take it to the hospital. She was locked into a cell.

Several weeks passed before the trial was held. Lalla Aïcha had been discharged from the hospital and gone home to find the empty house. She received the bad news about Sadek and Fatoma with no show of emotion, save that she shook her head and murmured: It was written.

She doesn't understand what has happened, they whispered behind her back. It's too much for her, poor thing.

They brought her food each day so she would not have to go to the market. Instead of climbing up to her room to sleep, Lalla Aïcha installed herself downstairs in the matrimonial bedroom, explaining to the neighbours that by the time Sadek and Fatoma came home she would be entirely recovered from her operation, and could then climb the stairs with more ease.

She still doesn't realize, they told one another.

At the trial Fatoma testified that she had given Sadek the basket with the food in it, but that she knew nothing about any poison.

Yet you admit that the tajine came from your kitchen.

Of course, said Fatoma. I was there while the old woman was making it. The afternoon before she went to the hospital she put everything together the way she likes her tajine. She told me to cook it the next day and have Sadek take it to her in the hospital.

This struck the court as an unlikely tale. It was decided to adjourn and call in Lalla Aïcha at the next session.

The old woman arrived on the witness stand entirely covered in her haïk. She was asked to remove it from around her head so they could hear what she was saying. Then they were startled to hear her declare with a note of pride in her voice that indeed she had made the tajine with her own hands. Yes, yes, she said. I like to use lots of marinated lemons.

And what else did you put into it? the qadi asked in a deceptively gentle voice.

Lalla Aïcha began the recital of a list of ingredients. Then she stopped and said: Do you want the whole recipe?

Everyone laughed. The qadi called for silence, and fixing her with a baleful stare, said: I see. We have a humorist with us. Sit down. We'll come back to you later.

Lalla Aïcha sat and looked into her lap, murmuring as she told the beads on her chaplet. The qadi glared at her from time to time, incensed by her unconcern. He was waiting for a report from some special police who had been left behind in Sadek's house when Lalla Aïcha had been brought in. It came soon enough. Upstairs in her closet among her clothes they had come across a half-empty container of the same rat-killer that had been found in the tajine.

The qadi's expression was triumphant when he next called Lalla Aïcha to the stand. In his left hand he held a tin box which he shook in front of her face. Have you ever seen this box? he demanded.

Lalla Aïcha did not hesitate. Of course I've seen it. It belongs to me. That's what I used in the tajine.

The sound of whispering moved through the chamber: the spectators had decided that the old woman was feeble-minded. For an instant the qadi's eyes and mouth opened wide. Then he frowned.

Ah, you admit that it was you who put the poison into the tajine?

Lalla Aïcha sighed. I asked you if you wanted the recipe, and you didn't. I put half a kilo of lemons in. It covers up the taste of the powder.

Go on, said the qadi, looking fixedly at her.

That was special food for me, she continued, a note of indignation in her voice. Not for anybody else. It was medicine. You don't think I was going to eat it, do you? I wanted to let the poison in the tajine draw out the poison in my body.

I don't know what you're talking about, the qadi told her.

You put it into your mouth and spit it out. Then you put more in and spit it out, and keep doing it, and you wash your mouth out with water in between. That's an old medicine from my tchar. It gets rid of all the poison.

Don't you know you killed a woman with your nonsense?

Lalla Aïcha shook her head. No, no. It was written, that's all.

From another part of the chamber came Fatoma's shrill voice: Lies! It's not true! She knew they weren't going to let the food in! She knew before she went to the hospital!

Fatoma was silenced. The qadi, nevertheless, made a note, and the following day when she was called to the witness stand, he asked her to elaborate. As a result of Fatoma's tale, they next called in Lalla Halima, the neighbour from across the street. She too had to be asked to loosen her haïk, which she did with visible distaste.

Two, maybe three days before Lalla Aïcha was going to

leave for the hospital, I went to see her. I wanted to be good to her, so I said: I'm going to have my daughter make some cabrozels and maybe some mrozeiya, and take them around to you in the hospital. She said: That's very kind of you, but it's no use. They have a new law, so the doctor told me, and they don't let anything in from the outside. So I had my daughter make some cabrozels anyway, and I took them to her myself the night before she went. I thought maybe she could wrap her clothes around them and put them into her bag, and they wouldn't see them.

That's all, said the qadi, making a gesture of dismissal. His eyes glittered as he said to Lalla Aïcha: And now what are you going to tell me?

I've told you everything, she said calmly. I was very busy trying to get my medicine made, and I forgot they wouldn't let it in. I'm an old woman. It went out of my head.

There was a commotion in one corner of the hall as Fatoma screamed: She didn't forget! She knew Sadek would leave it at my mother's!

Fatoma was hustled out of the court, still shouting and struggling. Lalla Aïcha stood quietly, waiting to be addressed. The qadi merely looked at her, an expression of doubt on his face.

Finally he said with exasperation: You're a stupid, ignorant woman. Who ever heard of poison in the mouth absorbing poison in the blood? Do you think anyone believes that nonsense?

Lalla Aïcha was unmoved. Yes, she said patiently. Everybody knows that Nazarene medicine works better if you take Moslem medicine at the same time. The power of Allah is very great.

In despair the qadi dismissed the case and sent the three defendants home, after warning Sadek that he would be held responsible for any further trouble caused by his mother, since she was clearly not responsible for her actions.

That night, when Lalla Aïcha was asleep in her room upstairs, Fatoma presented Sadek with an ultimatum. Either he sent his mother away, or she would leave him and go to live with her father.

She killed my mother. I won't stay in the house with her.

Sadek was wise enough to accept this; he offered no objection. In the light of what she had done, he himself had come to the conclusion that it would be better to take his mother back to the country to live with the rest of her family.

She received the news quietly; indeed, she seemed to have been expecting it. In the hope of persuading her that he was not being arbitrary, was not merely getting rid of her, he added: You see what your foolishness has done.

Then she faced him and looked into his eyes. You have no right to blame me for anything, she told him. It's not my fault if you're still living in this little house.

At the time the remark meant nothing to him; it was merely a senile non-sequitur. Later, when he had returned from the tchar in the valley and was living quietly with Fatoma, he recalled it. After that, he often thought about it.

Mejdoub

A man who spent his nights sleeping in cafés or under the trees or wherever he happened to be at the time when he felt sleepy, wandered one morning through the streets of the town. He came to the market place, where an old mejdoub dressed in rags cavorted before the populace, screaming prophecies into the air. He stood watching until the old man had finished and gathered up the money the people offered him. It astonished him to see how much the madman had collected, and having nothing else to do, he decided to follow him.

Almost before he got out of the market he was aware that small boys were hurrying from under the arcades to run alongside the mejdoub, who merely strode forward, chanting and waving his sceptre, and from time to time threatening the children who came too close. Walking at some distance behind, he saw the old man go into several shops. He came out each time with a banknote in his hand, which he promptly gave to one of the small boys.

It occurred to him then that there was much he could learn from this mejdoub. He had only to study the old man's behaviour and listen carefully to the words he uttered. Then with practice he himself could make the same gestures and shout the same words. He began to look each day for the mejdoub and to follow him wherever he went in the town. At the end of a month he decided that he was ready to put his knowledge to use.

He travelled south to another city where he had never gone before. Here he took a very cheap room by the slaughterhouse, far from the centre of town. In the flea-market he bought an old and tattered djellaba. Then he went to the ironmongers and stood watching while they made him a long sceptre like the one the mejdoub had carried.

The next day, after practising for a while, he went into the town and sat down in the street at the foot of the largest mosque. For a while he merely looked at the people going past. Slowly he began to raise his arms to the sky, and then to gesture with them. No one paid him any attention. This reassured him, as it meant that his disguise was successful. When he began to shout words the passers-by looked toward him, but it was as if they could not see him, and were only waiting to hear what he had to say. For a time he shouted short quotations from the Koran. He moved his eyes in a circular motion and let his turban fall over his face. After crying the words *fire* and *blood* several times he lowered his arms and bent his head, and said no more. The people moved on, but not before many of them had tossed coins on the ground in front of him.

On succeeding days he tried other parts of the city. It did not seem to matter where he sat. The people were generous to him in one place the same as in another. He did not want to risk going into the shops and cafés until he was certain that the town had grown used to his presence. One day he stormed through the streets, shaking his sceptre to the sky and screaming: Sidi Rahal is here! Sidi Rahal tells you to prepare for the fire! This was in order to give himself a name for the townspeople to remember.

He began to stand in the doorways of shops. If he heard anyone refer to him as Sidi Rahal, he would step inside, glare at the proprietor, and without saying a word, hold out his hand. The man would give him money, and he would turn and walk out.

For some reason no children followed him. He would have been happier to have a group of them with him, like the old mejdoub, but as soon as he spoke to them, they were frightened and ran away. It's quieter like this, he told himself, but secretly it bothered him. Still, he was earning more money than he ever had thought possible. By the time the first rains arrived, he had saved up a large sum. Leaving his sceptre and ragged djellaba in his room by the slaughterhouse, he paid the landlord several months' rent in advance. He waited until night. Then he locked the door behind him and took a bus back to his own city.

First he bought a great variety of clothing. When he was richly dressed he went out and looked for a house. Soon he found one that suited him. It was small and he had enough money left to pay for it. He furnished two rooms and prepared to spend the winter eating and smoking kif with all his old friends.

When they asked him where he had been all summer, he spoke of the hospitality and generosity of his wealthy brother in Taza. Already he was impatient for the rains to stop. For there was no doubt that he truly enjoyed his new work.

The winter finally came to an end. He packed his bag and told his friends that he was going on a business trip. In the other town he walked to the room. His djellaba and sceptre were there.

This year many more people recognized him. He grew bolder and entered the shops without waiting in the doorways. The shopkeepers, eager to show their piety to the customers, always gave a good deal more than the passers-by.

One day he decided to make a test. He hailed a taxi. As he got in he bellowed: I must go to Sidi Larbi's tomb! Fast! The driver, who knew he was not going to be paid, nevertheless agreed, and they rode out to a grove of olive trees on a hill far from the town.

He told the driver to wait, and jumped out of the taxi. Then he began the long climb up the hill to the tomb. The driver lost patience and drove off. On the way back to the town he missed a curve and hit a tree. When he was let out of the hospital he spread the word that Sidi Rahal had caused the car to go off the road. Men talked at length about it, recalling other holy maniacs who had put spells on motors and brakes. The name of

Sidi Rahal was on everyone's lips, and people listened respectfully to his rantings.

That summer he amassed more money than the year before. He returned home and bought a larger house to live in, while he rented out the first one. Each year he bought more houses and lands, until finally it was clear that he had become a very prosperous man.

Always when the first rains fell he would announce to his friends that he was about to travel abroad. Then he would leave secretly, never allowing anyone to see him off. He was delighted with the pattern of his life, and with the good luck he had been granted in being able to continue it. He assumed that Allah did not mind if he pretended to be one of His holy maniacs. The money was merely his reward for providing men with an opportunity to exercise their charity.

One winter a new government came to power and announced that all beggars were to be taken off the streets. He talked about this with his friends, all of whom thought it an excellent thing. He agreed with them, but the news kept him from sleeping at night. To risk everything by going back, merely because that was what he wanted to do, was out of the question. Sadly he resigned himself to spending the summer at home.

It was not until the first few weeks of spring had gone by that he realized how close it had been to his heart, the starting out on a fine starry night to go in the bus to the other city, and what a relief it had been each time to be able to forget everything and live as Sidi Rahal. Now he began to understand that his life here at home had been a pleasure only because he had known that at a certain moment he was going to leave it for the other life.

As the hot weather came on he grew increasingly restless. He was bored and lost his appetite. His friends, noticing the change in him, advised him to travel, as he always had done. They said that men had been known to die as a result of breaking a habit. Again he lay awake at night worrying, and then secretly he determined to go back. As soon as he had made the decision he felt much better. It was as though until then he had been asleep, and suddenly had awakened. He announced to his friends that he was going abroad.

That very night he locked up his house and got onto a bus. The next day he strode joyously through the streets to sit in his favourite spot by the mosque. Passers-by looked at him and remarked to one another: He's back again, after all. You see?

He sat there quietly all day, collecting money. At the end of the afternoon, since the weather was very hot, he walked down to the river outside the gates of the town, in order to bathe. As he was undressing behind some oleander bushes, he glanced up and saw three policemen coming down the bank toward him. Without waiting he seized his slippers, threw his djellaba over his shoulder, and began to run.

Sometimes he splashed into the water, and sometimes he slipped in the mud and fell. He could hear the men shouting after him. They did not chase him very far, for they were laughing. Not knowing this, he kept on running, following the river, until he was breathless and had to stop. He put on the djellaba and the slippers, thinking: I can't go back to the town, or to any other town, in these clothes.

He continued at a slower gait. When evening came he was hungry, but there were no people or houses in sight. He slept under a tree, with only the ragged djellaba to cover him.

The next morning his hunger had grown. He got up, bathed in the river, and set out again. All that day he walked under the hot sun. In the late afternoon he sat down to rest. He drank a little water from the river and looked around him at the countryside. On the hill behind him stood a partially ruined shrine.

When he was rested, he climbed up to the building. There was a tomb inside, in the centre of the big domed room. He sat down and listened. Cocks crowed, and he heard the occasional barking of dogs. He imagined himself running to the village, crying to the first man he met: Give me a piece of bread, for the love of Moulay Abdelqader! He shut his eyes.

It was nearly twilight when he awoke. Outside the door

stood a group of small boys, watching him. Seeing him awaken, they laughed and nudged one another. Then one boy tossed in a piece of dry bread, so that it fell beside him. Soon they were all chanting: He's eating bread! He's eating bread!

They played the game for a while, throwing in clods of earth and even uprooted plants along with scraps of bread. In their faces he could read wonder, malice and contempt, and shining through these shifting emotions the steady gleam of ownership. He thought of the old mejdoub, and a shiver ran through him. Suddenly they had gone. He heard a few shrill cries in the distance as they raced back to the village.

The bread had given him a little nourishment. He slept where he was, and before it grew light he set out again along the river, giving thanks to Allah for having allowed him to get beyond the village without being seen. He understood that heretofore the children had run from him only because they knew that he was not ready for them, that they could not make him theirs. The more he thought about this, the more fervently he hoped never to know what it was like to be a true mejdoub.

That afternoon as he turned a bend in the river, he came suddenly upon a town. His desperate need for food led him straight to the market, paying no heed to the people's stares. He went into a stall and ordered a bowl of soup. When he had finished it and paid, he entered another stall for a dish of stew. In a third place he ate skewered meat. Then he walked to the bread market for two loaves of bread to carry with him. While he was paying for these, a policeman tapped him on the shoulder and asked for his papers. He had none. There was nothing to say. At the police station they locked him into a small foul-smelling room in the cellar. Here in this closet he passed four days and nights of anguish. When at the end of that time they took him out and questioned him, he could not bring himself to tell them the truth. Instead he frowned, saying: I am Sidi Rahal.

They tied his hands and pushed him into the back of a truck. Later in the hospital they led him to a damp cell where the men stared and shivered and shrieked. He bore it for a week, and then he decided to give the officials his true name. But when he asked to be taken before them, the guards merely laughed. Sometimes they said: Next week, but usually they did not answer at all.

The months moved by. Through nights and days and nights he lived with the other madmen, and the time came when it scarcely mattered to him any more, getting to the officials to tell them who he was. Finally he ceased thinking about it.

The Dismissal

It was not his fault that he had lost his job, Abdelkrim explained to his friends. For more than a year and a half he had worked at Patricia's, and they always had got on smoothly. This is not to say that she did not find fault with him; but Nazarenes always criticize the work Moslems do for them, and he was used to that. Although at such moments she looked at him as though he were a small child, her objections came out in a gentler voice that most Nazarenes use. His tasks were simple enough, but they had demanded his constant presence on the property. Unless he were given specific permission to go to the cinema or sit in a café for an hour or two, he was obliged to be on hand. Patricia relied solely upon taxis; she had no car, so that Abdelkrim was able to live comfortably in the garage, where he cooked his own meals and listened to his radio.

Patricia had come from California a few years ago and bought the house. She was not exactly a girl, because she told him she had already been married to three different men, but she looked like a girl, and behaved, he said, like a nervous virgin who suspected she was never going to find a husband. I swear, he said, you wouldn't think she'd ever had a man.

She wore peculiar clothes, and pounds of jangling jewelry (it was all silver and copper, he said, not gold). Even her long earrings made a constant clicking sound. Abdelkrim's feeling about her was that she was a nice girl, but crazier than most Nazarenes. Even when the weather was not cold she wanted a fire roaring in the fireplace. There were plenty of electric lights, but she would only burn candles; she said electricity gave a dead light. The house was crammed with zebra hides and leopard pelts, and there was a collection of monstrous wooden heads which she claimed were African gods. Abdelkrim could see for himself that they represented devils. He always looked past them rather than at them.

For the six months prior to his dismissal Patricia's mother had been staying with her. She was a small excitable woman with bulging black eyes. In her frequent arguments with Patricia she shrieked and sometimes wept, and he decided that it was her mother who had made Patricia crazy.

Abdelkrim's job consisted of three distinct kinds of work. In the morning he had to walk two miles to the market in the city, buy the food for the day and carry it back to the house. Afternoons he worked in the garden, and at night he acted as watchman. Patricia had presented her terms at the beginning, and he had accepted them. Since then he had never been absent for an hour without permission.

It was not a good garden to be in on a hot afternoon. Since the house was new, there was not one bush or tree big enough to provide any shade. Abdelkrim did not mind working in the sun, but he liked to rest fairly often and smoke a pipe of kif, and in order for that to give him the greatest relaxation and pleasure, he must be sitting somewhere deep in the shade. As a boy fifteen years ago, he had known shady places nearby where he and his friends played. He had vivid memories of the pine woods at Moujahiddine, the grove of high eucalyptus trees that covered the hillside at Ain Chqaf, and the long shaded tunnels the boys cut through the jungle of matted vines and blackberry bushes outside his house. All this was gone now; new villas covered the countryside.

There did remain one place where he could find the sort of shade he had loved to seek out in his boyhood. Half an hour's walk from Patricia's house, around the long cemetery wall, over the fields, and down into the valley of Boubana, took him to the country club, nestling in an oasis of greenery. Behind the clubhouse lay a strip of the original forestland, with a slow-moving stream that meandered noiselessly through it. The golf course was more often than not deserted; he could run across the fairways without fear of being seen, and then follow the stream until he came to the forest. Where the big trees began, it was like entering a huge silent building. The screaming of the cicadas was left outside with the sunlight. Once inside, all he could hear was the stirring of leaves in the upper branches, a distant watery sound that seemed to him the perfect music for a hot summer afternoon.

One Friday Abdelkrim asked if he might be absent in the afternoon of the following day, since it was a national holiday. Without replying Patricia went into another room and began to confer with her mother. When she came out she said that they had been planning to go on a picnic with some American friends, but that they could arrange to go on Sunday just as well.

Saturday came up hot and still. Since there was to be a parade, his friends had gone off to the town to see it. When Abdelkrim had carried the food back from the market and left it in the kitchen, he went quietly to his room in the garage. There he put his bread, tunafish and olives into a small bag, along with everything else that would help him to pass a pleasant afternoon, and went out through the gate bound for Boubana. Probably he would not have undertaken the long walk in the heat of the day (for it was unusually hot) if only there had been a dark corner of the garden where he could have sat and smoked and drunk his tea in shadowed privacy. This sun is poison, he said to himself as he went along.

When he entered the forest he was already hungry. Not far from one of the paths that snaked through the underbrush, he found a large flat rock where he spread out his things and ate a leisurely lunch. This is the place to be, he thought, not standing in the sun on the Boulevard along with fifty thousand others, waiting to see a few floats go past. He smoked a few pipes of kif, and laying his sebsi beside him on the rock, he yawned, leaned back, and stretched. At that moment he became aware of a commotion in the bushes on the other side of the stream. There were grunts and wheezes, and then a heavy thud as something hit the ground. He remained immobile for an instant, then swiftly threw himself face downward, flat on the earth.

The sounds came closer. He raised his head a bit and saw, not far away, five men carrying a big black cube as they stumbled along the path among the trees. In another instant he knew that the object, which seemed to be almost too heavy for them to manage, was a safe. There was a crackling sound as they dropped it into a mass of bushes. Rapidly they uprooted plants and gathered armfuls of leaves, tossing them in piles, to cover all signs of the object.

With great caution Abdelkrim crawled in the opposite direction, still flat on his belly. A dry branch cracked under him as he slid across it. The sounds of activity behind him ceased. A voice said: Someone's there.

Then he got to his feet wildly and ran. At one point he made the mistake of looking back. The five men stood there, staring after him. But he had recognized one of them, and in turn had been recognized.

He ran panting out of the woods, across a field, and into a lane bordered by thorn bushes. Three farmers were stretched out under a tree, eyeing him with surprise. He slowed his pace. When he was out of their sight he pulled off his sweat-soaked shirt. The police might easily question the farmers.

He was now certain that no one was following him. He got to the paved road, where an occasional car went by, and breathed more easily.

What he had seen in that brief instant of looking back was the brutal face of Aziz, the waiter in the bar at the country club. Everyone feared and disliked him, but the director kept him working there because one blow of his huge fist on the top of the head landed a troublesome client on the floor. They said of Aziz, and only half in jest, that the only times he prayed were just after he had killed someone.

If the farmers should mention that they had seen a young man hurrying along the lane, the police could find him and ask him questions, and no matter what he told them, if Aziz were caught, he would never believe it had not been Adbelkrim who had betrayed him.

It was even hotter once he had crossed the bridge and started to climb the hill. He had heard enough about Aziz to know that the most prudent thing for him to do at the moment was to get out of Tangier. His brother Mustapha would be happy to see him. Agadir was a long way off, but once he was there he would have no expenses.

He walked to the house with the afternoon sun beating down on his back. In the garage he threw himself onto the mattress and thought about his bad luck. His kif, his pipe, everything he had taken with him to the woods, had remained behind, there on the rock.

He would catch the night bus for Casablanca, the one that left the beach at half past eleven. Patricia and her mother must suspect nothing; indeed, his main consideration was how to get out of the garage and through the big gate without their hearing him, for at night the only sounds near the house came from the crickets. If one of them were to hear the gate click behind him when he crept out, he knew they would rush out and go screaming along the road after him in their bathrobes.

Soon Patricia knocked on the door, interrupting his meditations. I thought I heard you come in, she said with satisfaction. Afraid that his disturbed state might somehow show in his face, he forced himself to smile, but she did not notice because she had more to say. They had been invited by Monsieur and Madame Lemoine to attend a Jilala party at half past seven, and he could come too for a half hour if he wanted. It was to be at Hadj Larbi's house, which was not far away, so that it would be easy for him to walk back before dark.

Abdelkrim nodded vigorously in agreement, an expression of unfeigned satisfaction on his face. He saw his problem being solved for him.

Now that he no longer dreaded the night, he was eager for it to arrive. The suitcase he would take with him was ready; he hid it in a dark corner of the garage. At precisely half past seven Monsieur Lemoine was outside in the road, sounding his car horn; Madame Lemoine sat stiffly beside him. Patricia, loaded down with chains and medallions, ran to the car and leaned in to speak with Madame Lemoine. Now and then she raised her head and shouted the word Mother! toward the house.

Abdelkrim could hear the older woman complaining in her bedroom as she got her things together. Finally she came out, looking more irritable than usual. He sat between them on the back seat.

Hadj Larbi's garden was bounded at one end by a row of tall cypresses, black against the twilit sky. As they went in, one of Hadj Larbi's sons, whom Abdelkrim knew, came up to him and led him to the musicians' side of the courtyard. We have the Jilala in for my uncle every year during the smayyim, he told him.

Abdelkrim sat down on a mat beside the moqqaddem. An old man in a white djellaba came out of the house and stood facing the musicians. The drums began a leisurely rhythm, and he bent forward and slowly shuffled back and forth over the paving stones.

As the drummers increased their speed, the old man's feet ceased to scrape and drag; his legs now seemed to be springing upward of their own accord. He strained at the end of the sash that was wound about his waist and held by the man behind him. His eyes were on the fire, and he wanted to hurl himself into it. The music swelled in volume, the drummers began to hit the ground with the rims of their benadir, and the old man's frenzy increased. His face constantly changed its expression, distorted as if by waves of water washing over it. He was coming into the presence of the saint who would lead him far beyond the visible world to a place where his soul would be cleansed.

When he finally toppled to the ground there was a concerted rush of men to pull him away from the fire. They clustered around, touching his head, covering him with a blanket, lifting him carefully and carrying him away, out of sight.

Above the riad's wall Abdelkrim saw the dark obelisks of the cypresses. If he himself were to invoke Sidi Maimoun or Sidi

Rahal, he was certain they would pay him no attention; it was too late for young men to expect to get in touch with the saints. He slipped out into the garden, said good-night to a servant standing in the doorway, and was on his way.

At the garage he picked up his valise, locked the gate behind him, and set out for the bus terminal on the beach, trying not to imagine the scene that would ensue the next morning when they found him gone. He waited nearly three hours for the bus to open its doors and let the passengers in.

Two months later he had reliable word that Aziz and his accomplices had been caught the very day after the robbery, there in the same part of the woods while they hammered at the safe, trying to get it open. He returned to Tangier and went directly to Patricia's house. But a maid whom he did not know brought him word that she would not see him.

The maid's expression was apologetic; out of friendliness she added: The old one and the young one, they both say they'll never forgive you. The idea of this struck her as strangely comic, and she laughed.

Abdelkrim turned to look with scorn at the garden. More to himself than to her he said: One real tree, and it would have been different.

But in any case she had not heard him, or had not understood, for she continued to smile. No, they don't want to see you, she said again.

Here to Learn

I

Malika needed no one to tell her she was pretty. From the beginning of her memory people had murmured about her beauty, for even when she was a baby girl the symmetry of her head, neck and shoulders was remarkable. Before she was old enough to go to the spring to fetch water she knew she had eyes like a gazelle and that her head was like a lily on its stalk. At least, these were the things older people said about her.

On a hill above the town stood a large building with palm-shaded walks leading up to it. This belonged to the Hermanas Adoratrices. Certain of these nuns, upon catching sight of Malika, had gone to her father, offering to take her in charge and teach her to speak Spanish and to embroider. Enthusiastically he had agreed. Allah has sent us here to learn, he would say. Malika's mother, who disapproved of her daughter's spending her time with Nazarenes, did her utmost to make him change his mind. Nevertheless Malika stayed with the sisters for five years, until her father died.

Malika's grandmother was fond of saying that when she had been Malika's age she had looked exactly like her, and that if it were possible for her to become a little girl again and stand beside Malika, no one would be able to tell them apart. At first Malika found this impossible to believe; she studied the old woman's ravaged face and straightway rejected the idea. After her grandmother had died, she began to understand what the old woman had meant when she said: Only Allah remains the same. One day she would no longer be pretty, but now she was. Thus, when she was able to go by herself to the spring and carry back two full pails of water, it meant nothing to her if the older boys and the young men called to her and tried to speak with her. They would do better, she thought, to say all those flattering things to girls who needed such reassurance.

A barracks full of soldiers stood just outside the town. The men were rough and brutal. When she caught sight of one of them, even in the distance, Malika would hide until he had disappeared. Fortunately the soldiers seldom strayed into the arroyo that lay between her house and the spring; they preferred to saunter in groups up and down the main road leading through the town.

There came a day when her mother insisted that she go to sell a hen at the market on the main highway. Her older sister always had done this, but she was at a neighbour's house helping prepare for a wedding. Malika begged her mother to lend her her haïk so she could cover her face.

Your sister's been a thousand times. She never wears a haïk.

Malika knew this was because no one paid any attention to her sister, but she could not say it to her mother. I'm afraid, she said, and burst into tears. Her mother had no patience with the silly behaviour of girls, and refused to let her take the haïk. As Malika ran out of the house, holding the hen by its legs, she snatched up a soiled bathtowel. As soon as she was out of sight, she wrapped it loosely around her head, so that when she got to the highway she could pull it down and cover at least a part of her face.

Several dozen women lined one side of the road, each sitting on the ground with her wares spread out around her. Malika went to the end of the row, which was opposite a small park where the soldiers sat on benches. People wandered past and picked up the hen to squeeze it and shake it, so that it constantly squawked and fluttered. She had pulled the towel down so far over her eyes that she could see only the earth at her feet.

After an hour or so had gone by, a woman came along who

began to discuss the price of the hen with her. Eventually she bought it, and Malika, once she had tied the coins up in a piece of cloth, jumped to her feet. The towel slipped over her face and fell to the ground. She picked it up and started to hurry along the highway.

II

The town was derelict; it smelled of the poverty in which its people were accustomed to live. Nor was there any indication that in some past era something more had existed. The wind from the sea raised the dust of the streets high into the air and showered it angrily over the countryside. Even the leaves of the fig trees were coated white. The hot sand flying stung the skin on the backs of her legs as she turned the corner of the side street that led to the lower end of the gully. She draped the towel over her head and held onto it with one hand. It had never occurred to her to hate the town, for she assumed that anywhere else would be more or less the same.

The street was scarcely more than an alley, with walls on either side. All at once she heard the sound of heavy boots pounding the earth behind her. She did not turn around. Then a hard hand seized her arm and pushed her roughly against the wall. It was a soldier, and he was smiling. He braced his arms against the wall on each side of her so she could not escape.

Malika said nothing. The man stood gazing at her. He was breathing deeply, as though he had been running. Finally he said: How old are you?

She looked directly into his eyes. Fifteen.

He smelt of wine, tobacco and sweat.

Let me go, she said, and she tried desperately to duck under the barricade. The pain she felt as he twisted her arm made her open her eyes very wide, but she did not cry out. Two men in djellabas were approaching from the direction of the gully, and she fixed her eyes on them. The soldier turned, saw them, and began to walk quickly back toward the highway.

When she got home, she tossed the bit of cloth with the money in it onto the taifor, and indignantly showed her mother the marks on her arm.

What's that?

A soldier grabbed me.

Her mother dealt her a stinging blow across the face. Malika had never seen her in such a rage.

You young bitch! she screamed. That's all you're good for!

Malika ran out of the house and down into the gully, where she sat on a rock in the shade, wondering if her mother might be going mad. The unexpectedness and injustice of the sudden blow had removed all thought of the soldier from her mind. She felt that she must find an explanation of her mother's behaviour; otherwise she would hate her.

That night at dinner things were not much better; her mother would not look at her, and directed all her remarks to her other daughter. This proved to be the pattern for the days that followed. It was as if she had decided that Malika no longer existed.

Good, thought Malika. If I'm not here, then she's not here. She's not my mother and I do hate her.

This silent war between them did not mean that Malika was exempt from having to continue to go to the market. Nearly every week she would be sent off to sell a hen or a basket of vegetables and eggs. She had no further trouble with the soldiers, perhaps because she now stopped on her way down the gully each time and smeared a little mud over her face. It was always dry by the time she reached the highway, and although the women there sometimes stared at her with surprise, the men paid her no attention. On her way home, going up the gully, she would wash her face.

There was always suspicion in her mother's glance now when she returned to the house. If you get into trouble, she said, I swear I'll kill you with my own hands. Malika sniffed and left the room. She knew what her mother meant, but it astonished her to see how little she knew about her own daughter.

III

One day as Malika sat in the front row of women and girls in the market on the highway, a long yellow car without a top drove up silently and stopped. There was only one man in it, and he was a Nazarene. The women began to murmur and cry out, for the man held a camera in his hands and was pointing it at them. A girl sitting next to Malika turned to her and said: You speak Spanish. Tell him to go away.

Malika ran over to the car. The man lowered his camera and stared at her.

Señor, you mustn't take pictures here, she said, looking at him gravely. She pointed back at the row of indignant women.

The Nazarene was big, with light-coloured hair. He understood and smiled. *Muy bien, muy bien,* he said good-naturedly, still looking fixedly at her. She was suddenly conscious of the dirt on her face. Without thinking she rubbed her cheek with the back of her hand. The man's smile became broader.

Will you let me take your picture?

Malika's heart began to beat painfully. No! No! she cried, aghast. Then by way of explanation she added: I have to go and sell my eggs.

The Nazarene looked more pleased than ever. You have eggs for sale? Bring them over.

Malika went and fetched the little packet of eggs, tied in a cloth. A group of boys had caught sight of the dazzling yellow car, and now they surrounded it, demanding money. The Nazarene, trying to wave them away, opened the door for Malika and pointed to the empty seat. She laid the bundle on the leather cushion and bent to undo the knot, but the arms of the boys kept pushing in front of her and jostling her. The Nazarene shouted angrily at the urchins in a foreign language, but this deterred them only for an instant. Finally, in a rage, he said to Malika: Get in. She lifted the eggs and obeyed, seating herself with the bundle on her lap. The man reached in front of her and slammed the door shut. Then he raised the window.

But two beggars now had joined the boys, and they were able to reach over the top of the window.

Without warning the Nazarene started up the motor with a great roar. The car shot forward. Startled, Malika turned to see some of the boys sprawling in the road. When she looked again, they were almost out of the town. The Nazarene still seemed to be very angry. She decided not to ask him how far he was going before he stopped and bought the eggs. Her emotions hovered between delight at being in the fine car and anxiety about walking back to the town.

The trees were going by very fast. It seemed to her that she had always known something strange like this would happen to her one day. It was a comforting thought, and it kept her from feeling actual fear.

IV

Soon they turned onto a dirt road that burrowed deep into a eucalyptus grove. Here in the dubious shade the Nazarene shut off the motor and turned to Malika with a smile. He took the bundle of eggs from her lap and put it into the back of the car. From a basket behind her seat he brought out a bottle of mineral water and a napkin. He poured a little water onto the napkin and with one hand on her shoulder set to work wiping the streaks of mud from her cheeks. She let him rub, and she let him remove the towel wrapped around her head, so that her hair fell to her shoulders. Why shouldn't he see me? she thought. He's a good man. She had already noticed that he did not smell at all, and his gentleness with her gave her a pleasant sensation.

Now shall I take your picture?

She nodded. There was no one to witness the shameful act. He made her sit lower in the seat, and held the camera above her. It clicked so many times, and he looked so peculiar with the big black apparatus in front of his face, that she began to laugh. She thought he might stop then, but he seemed even more pleased, and went on clicking the camera until it would click no more. Then he spread a blanket on the ground and set a basket of food in the centre of it. They sat with the basket between them and ate chicken, cheese and olives. Malika was hungry, and she thought this great fun.

When they had finished, he asked her if she wanted him to take her back to the market. It was as if darkness had fallen over the world. She thought of the women there, and of what they would say when they saw her. She shook her head vigorously. The present moment was real; she would not help it to end. No, not yet, she said lightly.

He looked at his watch. Shall we go to Tetuan?

Her eyes brightened. It was less than an hour's ride from her town, but she had only heard about it. The trees sped by again. Here a stiff breeze blew in from the Mediterranean, and Malika was chilly. The man took out a soft camel's-hair cape and put it around her shoulders.

Tetuan was very exciting with all its traffic. The guards in scarlet and white stood at attention in front of the Khalifa's palace. But she would not get out of the car and walk with him in the street. They were parked there in the Feddane, where the hot afternoon sun beat down on them. Finally the man shrugged and said: Well, if I'm going to get to Tangier tonight, I'd better take you back home.

Malika made a strange sound. She seemed to have become very small inside the cape.

What's the matter?

I can't!

The man stared at her. But you've got to go back home.

Malika began to wail. No, no! she cried. The man glanced nervously at the passers-by, and tried to comfort her with words. But a possibility had just revealed itself to her, and at that moment the idea was powerful enough to occupy her totally. Seeing her too immersed in inner turmoil even to hear him, he started the car and slowly made his way through the throng of people to the other side of the plaza. Then he drove along the principal street to the outskirts of the city, stopped the car by the side of the road, and lighted a cigarette.

He turned to her. One would almost have said that on the seat beside him there was nothing but the cape. He tugged at it, and heard a sob. Gently slipping his hand inside, he smoothed her hair for a moment. Finally she began to push herself upward into a sitting position, and her head appeared.

I'm going to take you with me to Tangier, he said. She made no reply to this, nor did she look at him.

They sped westward, the late afternoon sun in front of them. Malika was conscious of having made an irrevocable choice. The results, already determined by destiny, would be disclosed to her one by one, in the course of events. It was only slowly that she became aware of the landscape around her and of the summer air rushing past.

They came to a tiny café, alone on the mountainside, and stopped. Come in and we'll have some tea, he said. Malika shook her head, pulling the cape more tightly around her. The man went inside and ordered two glasses of tea. A quarter of an hour later a boy carried them to the car on a tray. The tea was very hot, and it took them a while to drink it. Even when the boy had come and taken away the tray, they went on sitting there. Eventually the man switched on the headlights, and they started down the mountainside.

V

Malika was frightened by the elevator, but she relaxed somewhat when the man had shown her into the apartment and shut the door behind them. There were thick rugs and soft couches piled with pillows, and lights that could be turned on and off by pushing a button. Most important of all, the Nazarene lived there by himself.

That night he showed her to a room, telling her it was to be hers. Before he said good-night he took her head in his hands and kissed her on the forehead. When he had gone she wandered into the bathroom and amused herself for a long time turning the hot and cold taps on and off, to see if sooner or later one of them would make a mistake. Finally she undressed, put on the muslin gandoura the man had left for her, and got into the bed.

A pile of magazines lay on the table beside her, and she began to look at the pictures. There was one photograph which caught her attention and held it. The picture showed a luxurious room, with a beautiful woman lying back in a chaise longue. A wide collar of diamonds flashed from her neck, and in her hand she held a book. The book was open but she was not looking at it. Her head was raised, as though someone had just come into the room and found her reading. Malika studied the photograph, glanced at others, and returned to it. To her it illustrated the perfect pose to adopt when receiving guests, and she resolved to practise it by herself, so that when the time came she could put it to use. It would be a good idea to be able to read, too, she thought. One day she would ask the man to show her how.

They had breakfast on the terrace in the morning sun. The building overlooked a spacious Moslem cemetery. Beyond it was the water. Malika told him it was not good to live so near to a graveyard. Later, she looked over the railing, saw the elaborate domed mausoleum of Sidi Bou Araqia, and nodded her head in approval. As they sat over their coffee, he answered more of her questions. His name was Tim, he was twenty-eight years old, but he had no wife and no children. He did not live in Tangier all the time. Sometimes he was in Cairo and sometimes in London. In each of these places he had a small flat, but he kept his car in Tangier because that was where he came when he was not working.

As they sat there Malika heard sounds inside the apartment. Presently a fat black woman in a yellow zigdoun came onto the terrace. *Bonjour*, she said, and she began to carry out the dishes. Each time she appeared Malika sat very straight, looking fixedly out across the water at the mountains in Spain.

Someone would be coming in a little while, Tim said, an

Italian woman who was going to take her measurements and make some clothes for her.

Malika frowned. What kind of clothes?

When he said: Whatever you want, she jumped up and went to her room, returning with a copy of *The New Yorker*, which she opened at a page showing a girl in a knit sports suit standing by a set of matched luggage. Like this one, she said. An hour or so later the Italian woman came in, very businesslike, tickled Malika with her tape measure for a while, and left, notebook in hand.

VI

Late that afternoon when the black woman had gone, Tim took Malika into her bedroom, pulled the curtains across the windows, and very gently gave her her first lesson in love. Malika did not really want this to happen then, but she had always known it would sooner or later. The slight pain was negligible, but the shame of being naked in front of the man was almost more than she could bear. It never had occurred to her that a body could be considered beautiful, and she did not believe him when he told her she was perfect in every part. She knew only that men used women in order to make children, and this preoccupied her, as she had no desire for a child. The man assured her that he was not hoping for children either, and that if she did as he told her there was no danger of having any. She accepted this as she accepted everything else he said. She was there in order to learn, and she intended to learn as much as possible.

When, during the next few weeks, she finally consented to go with him to the houses of his friends, he did not guess that she agreed to appear in public only because she had studied herself in the new clothes, and had found them sufficiently convincing to act as a disguise. The European garments made it possible for her to go into the streets with a Nazarene and not be reviled by other Moroccans.

After taking Malika to a photographer's studio and making several lengthy visits to the authorities, Tim returned triumphant one day, waving a passport at her. This is yours, he said. Don't lose it.

Nearly every day there were parties on the Mountain or picnics on the beach. Malika particularly loved the night picnics around a fire, with the sound of the waves breaking on the sand. Sometimes there were musicians, and everyone danced barefoot. One evening eight or ten of the guests jumped up and ran shouting toward the breakers to swim naked in the moonlight. Since the moon was very bright, and there were men and women together, Malika gasped and hid her face. Tim thought this amusing, but the incident caused her to question the fitness of the people in Tangier to be her models for the elegance she hoped to attain.

One morning Tim greeted her with a sad face. In a few days, he told her, he had to go to London. Seeing her expression of chagrin, he quickly added that in two weeks he would be back, and that she would go on living in the flat just as though he were there.

But how can I? she cried. You won't be here! I'll be all alone.

No, no. You'll have friends. You'll like them.

That evening he brought two young men to the apartment. They were handsome and well-dressed, and very talkative. When Malika heard Tim address one of them as Bobby, she burst into laughter.

Only dogs are called Bobby, she explained. It's not a man's name.

She's priceless, said Bobby. A teen-age Nefertiti.

Absolute heaven, agreed his friend Peter.

After they had gone, Tim explained that they were going to keep Malika company while he was in England. They would live in the apartment with her. On hearing this, she was silent for a moment.

I want to go with you, she said, as if anything else were inconceivable.

He shook his head. *Ni hablar.*

But I don't want love with them.

He kissed her. They don't make love with girls. That's why I asked them. They'll take good care of you.

Ah, she said, partially reassured, and at the same time thinking how clever Tim was to have been able to find two such presentable eunuchs with so little apparent effort.

As Tim had promised, Bobby and Peter kept her amused. Instead of taking her out to parties they invited their friends in to meet her. Soon she realized that there were a good many more eunuchs in Tangier than she had suspected. Since, according to Bobby and Peter, these tea-parties and cocktail hours were given expressly for Malika, she insisted on knowing exactly when the guests would be coming, so she could receive them in the correct position, lying back on the cushions of the divan with a book in her hand. When the new arrivals were shown in, she would raise her head slowly until its noble proportions were fully evident, fix her gaze on a point far behind anything in the room, and let the beginning of a smile tremble briefly on her lips before it vanished.

She could see that this impressed them. They told her they loved her. They played games and danced with each other and with her. They tickled her, nuzzled her, took her on their laps and fussed with her hair. She found them more fun to be with than Tim's friends, even though she was aware that the things they said had no meaning. To them everything was a game; there was nothing to learn from them.

VII

Tim had been gone for more than a week when they first brought Tony to the flat. He was a tall, noisy Irishman for whom the others of the group seemed to have a certain respect. At first Malika assumed that this was because he was not a eunuch like them, but quickly she discovered that it was only because he had far more money to spend than they did. Tony's clothing always smelled delicious, and his car, a green

Maserati, attracted even more attention than Tim's. One day he came by at noon, while Bobby and Peter were still at the market. The black woman had received orders from Bobby to let no one in under any circumstances, but Tony was an expert in getting around such things. Malika had been playing a record of Abdelwahab's; now she quickly silenced it and gave all her attention to Tony. In the course of their dialogue, he remarked casually that her clothes were pretty. Malika smoothed her skirt.

But I'd like to see you in some other clothes, he went on.

Where are they?

Not here. In Madrid.

They heard the door slam, and knew that Bobby and Peter had returned. The two had quarrelled and were communicating only in acid monosyllables. Malika saw that the game of dominoes they had promised to play with her when they got back would not take place. She sat and sulked for a while, turning the pages of one of Tim's financial magazines. Eunuchs were extremely childish, she reflected.

Bobby came into the room and stood at the other end, arranging books on the bookshelves in silence. Soon the black woman appeared in the doorway and announced to him in French that Monsieur Tim had telephoned from London and would not be in Tangier until the eighteenth.

When Tony had translated the information into Spanish, Malika merely sat staring at him, an expression of despair on her face.

Bobby hurried out of the room. Ill at ease, Tony stood up and followed him. A moment later Bobby's sharp voice cried: No, she can't go out to eat with you. She can't go out at all, anywhere, unless we go along. One of Tim's rules. If you want to eat here, you can.

Very little was said at lunch. In the middle of the meal Peter flung down his napkin and left the room. Afterward the black woman served coffee on the terrace. Bobby and Peter were arguing farther back in the flat, but their shrill voices were strangely audible.

For a while Malika sipped her coffee and said nothing. When she spoke to Tony, it was as if there had been no interruption to their earlier conversation. Can we go to Madrid? she said.

You'd like that? He grinned. But you see how they are. And he pointed behind him.

A mí me da igual cómo son. I only promised to stay with them for two weeks.

The next morning, while Bobby and Peter were at the market buying food, Tony and Malika put some valises into the Maserati and drove to the port to catch the ferry to Spain. Tony had left a short note for Bobby, saying that he had borrowed Malika for a few days, and would see to it that she telephoned.

VIII

They slept in Córdoba the first night. Before setting out for Madrid in the morning, Tony stopped at the cathedral to show it to her. When they walked up to the door, Malika hesitated. She peered inside and saw an endless corridor of arches extending into the gloom.

Go on in, said Tony.

She shook her head. You go. I'll wait here.

Driving out of the city, he scolded her a bit. You should look at things when you have the chance, he told her. That was a famous mosque.

I saw it, she said firmly.

The first day in Madrid they spent at Balenciaga's, morning and afternoon. You were right, Malika said to Tony when they were back in the hotel. The clothes here are much better.

They had to wait several days for the first items to be ready. The Prado was almost next door to the hotel, but Tony decided against making the attempt to entice Malika into it. He suggested a bullfight.

Only Moslems know how to kill animals, she declared.

They had been in Madrid for more than a week. One

evening as they sat in the bar downstairs at the Ritz, Tony turned to her and said: Have you called Tangier? No, you haven't. Come.

Malika did not want to think of Tangier. Sighing, she rose and went with Tony up to his room, where he put in the call. When finally he heard Bobby at the other end of the wire, he gestured and handed the telephone to Malika.

At the sound of her voice, Bobby immediately began to reproach her. She interrupted him to ask for Tim.

Tim can't get back to Tangier quite yet, he said, and the pitch of his voice rose as he added: But he wants *you* to come back right now!

Malika was silent.

Did you hear what I said? yelled Bobby. *Oíste?*

Yes, I heard. I'll let you know. She hung up quickly so as not to hear the sounds of outraged protest at the other end.

They went several more times to Balenciaga for fittings. Malika was impressed by Madrid, but she missed the comforting presence of Tim, particularly at night when she lay alone in her bed. While it was pleasant to be with Tony because he paid so much attention to her and constantly bought her gifts, she knew he did this only because he enjoyed dressing her the way he wanted her to look when they went out together, and not because he cared about her.

Although the deliveries continued to be made, and the gowns and ensembles were perfect, Malika's pleasure was somewhat lessened by her discovery that the only places where people really looked at what she was wearing were two restaurants and the bar downstairs. When she remarked about this to Tony, he laughed.

Ah! What you want is Paris. I can see that.

Malika brightened. Can we go there?

When the last garment had arrived, Tony and Malika ate a final dinner at Horcher, and started early the next morning for Paris. They spent the night in Biarritz, where the streets were rainswept and empty.

IX

Paris was far too big. She was frightened of it even before they arrived at the hotel, and she determined not to let Tony out of her sight unless she was safe in her room. At the Hôtel de la Trémoaille she watched him lying back on his bed, making one telephone call after the other while he joked, shouted, waved his legs, and screamed with laughter. When he was through telephoning he turned to her.

Tomorrow night I'm going to take you to a party, he said. And I know just what you'll wear. The oyster-coloured satin number.

Malika was excited by the sumptuous house and the guests in evening clothes. Here at last, she was certain, she had reached a place where the people were of the ultimate degree of refinement. When she found that they looked at her with approval, she was filled with a sense of triumph.

Soon Tony led her up to a tall, pretty girl with flashing black eyes. This is my sister Dinah, he announced. She speaks better Spanish than I do.

Indicating Malika, he added: and this is the new Antinea. He left the two together and disappeared into another room.

Dinah's manner with her made her feel that they had been friends for a long time. When they had chatted for a few minutes, she led her over to a group of South Americans. The women were covered with jewels and some of them carried the pelts of animals over their shoulders. Even the men wore huge diamonds on their fingers. Malika suspected that Tim would disapprove of these people, but then it occurred to her that perhaps he could not be relied upon as an arbiter of taste in a city like this.

Paris es muy grande, she said to a man who smiled at her invitingly. I never saw it until yesterday. I'm afraid to go out. Why did they make it so big?

The man, smiling more broadly, said he was at her service, and would be delighted to go with her wherever she wished, whenever it suited her.

Oh, she said, looking pensive. That would be nice.
Mañana?

Somehow Dinah had caught the end of their dialogue. Not
tomorrow, I'm afraid, she said briskly, taking Malika's arm.
As she led her away she whispered furiously: His wife was
standing there watching you.

Malika stole a frightened glance over her shoulder. The man
was still smiling after her.

During the next few days Dinah, who lived nearby in the
Avenue Montaigne, came regularly to the hotel. She and Tony
had long discussions while Malika listened to Radio Cairo.
One afternoon when Tony had gone out and Malika was
bored, she asked Dinah to put in a call to Bobby in Tangier. A
half hour later the telephone rang, and she heard Bobby's voice.

Hola, Bobby!

Malika! His voice was already shrill. You can't do this to me!
Why are you in Paris? You've got to come back to Tangier.

Malika was silent.

We're waiting for you. What will Tim say if you're not here?

Tim! she said with scorn. Where is Tim?

He's coming back next week. I want to speak to Tony.

Tony's gone out.

Listen to me! Bobby shouted. What hotel are you in?

I don't know its name, she said. It's in Paris. It's a nice hotel.
Adiós.

One morning not long afterward Tony announced abruptly
that he was leaving for London in an hour. Dinah came in
shortly before he set out. They seemed to be involved in a
dispute, which ended only when he kissed each of them good-
bye. After he had gone, Malika nodded her head sagely.
London, she mused. He won't come back.

X

The day after Malika moved into Dinah's flat the weather
turned rainy and cold. Dinah often went out, leaving her alone

with the housemaid and cook. She was just as glad to stay indoors where it was warm. Her wardrobe, impressive as it was, failed to include any kind of covering for cold weather. Dinah had told her that the cold was just beginning, and that it would not be warm again for many months. It seemed to Malika that somewhere in Paris there must be a *joteya*, where she could take two or three evening gowns and exchange them for a coat, but Dinah shook her head when she asked her about it.

The apartment was spacious, and there were plenty of magazines to study. Malika spent her time curled up on a divan, examining the details in the fashion photographs.

Tony called from London, postponing his return for a few days. When Dinah gave her the news, Malika smiled and said: *Claro.*

I'm having lunch today with a friend. She has mountains of clothes, said Dinah. I'll see if I can't get a coat for you.

What she brought back that afternoon was a mink coat badly in need of repairs. Malika gazed at the rips with visible distaste.

You haven't any idea of how lucky you are, Dinah told her. She shrugged.

When the garment had been fitted at the furrier's and the skins resewn, it looked completely new, as if it had just been made for Malika. She ran her fingers over its glistening surface and examined herself in the mirror, and quickly decided that it was a very fine coat after all.

Dinah's friend came to lunch. Her name was Daphne. She was not very pretty and she tried to speak Italian with Malika. During the course of the meal she invited them both to a house-party at Cortina d'Ampezzo.

Dinah was enthusiastic. She brought out an album of photographs after Daphne had left, and spread it in Malika's lap. Malika saw that the ground was white and the people, whose clothing was not at all elegant, wore long boards on their feet. She was doubtful, but the strange white landscape and the groups of festive people intrigued her. It might be more interesting than Paris, which in the end had turned out to be rather dull.

They went to the office to book plane passage. Have you any money at all? Dinah asked her as they waited.

Malika was suddenly very much ashamed. Tony never gave me any.

It's all right, Dinah told her.

Before they left there was a lively argument between them as to whether Malika should take all her valises with her on the plane to Milano.

But you won't need all those clothes there, Dinah objected. And besides, it would cost so much.

I have to take everything, Malika said.

All of her belongings went with them on the plane. They had bad weather on the way to Milano, where Daphne's car met them. She was already in Cortina.

Malika had not enjoyed the plane ride. She did not understand why people with cars took planes. There was nothing to see but clouds, and the rocking of the plane made some of the passengers sick, so that by the end of the flight everyone seemed to be nervous and unhappy. For a while as they sped along the autostrada Malika thought she was back in Spain.

According to the driver, there were already so many friends staying at Daphne's chalet that no place was left for them. Daphne was putting them up in a hotel. Dinah received this news in silence; presumably she was displeased. Malika, when she understood the situation, secretly rejoiced. There would be many more people in the hotel than in the house.

XI

It was cold in Cortina. At first Malika would not go out of the hotel. The air is like poison, she complained. Then she began to experiment a bit, finally discovering that it was an agreeable kind of cold.

She would sit with the others on the terrace of the hotel in the brilliant sunshine, wearing her warm coat, sipping hot chocolate while they had their cocktails. The red-cheeked jollity of the people around her was a new experience, and the snow never ceased to fascinate her. Each morning when Daphne and her guests came to fetch Dinah, Malika would watch the noisy group rush out toward the ski fields. Then she would wander through the public rooms. The employees were polite, and often smiled at her. There was a shop in the hotel that sold skis and the clothes that had to be worn when using them. The window displays were changed daily, so that Malika was often to be seen standing outside the door, inspecting the merchandise through the glass.

Twice a tall young man had sauntered up to the shop windows as she stood there, giving the impression that he was about to speak to her. Both times she had turned away and resumed her aimless meandering. Tony and Dinah had warned her repeatedly against entering into conversation with strangers, and she thought it better to observe the etiquette they considered so important. She had discovered that Otto the barman spoke Spanish, and in the morning when the bar was often empty she would go in and talk with him. One morning he asked her why she never went out to ski with her friends.

I can't, she said in a muffled voice.

At that moment, in the mirror behind the bar, she saw the tall young man come into the room and remain standing by the door, as if he were listening to their conversation. She hoped Otto would not continue it, but he did.

That's no reason, he said. Take lessons. There are plenty of good skiing professors in Cortina.

Malika shook her head slowly several times.

The young man stepped to the bar, saying, in Spanish: He's right, our friend Otto. That's what Cortina's for. Everybody skis here.

Now he leaned on the bar and faced Malika. I spend a lot of time south of the border myself, he said as though in confidence. I have a little hacienda down in Durango.

Malika stared at him. He was speaking in Spanish, but she had no idea of what he was talking about. He misunderstood her expression and frowned. What's the matter. Don't you like Durango?

She looked at Otto and back at the tall young man. Then she burst into laughter, and the sound filled the bar agreeably. The tall young man's face seemed to melt as he heard it.

She slid down from the barstool, smiled at him, and said: I don't understand. *Hasta luego*, Otto. While the young man was still making a visible effort to collect his thoughts, she turned and walked out of the bar.

This marked the beginning of a new friendship, one which grew to substantial proportions later that same day. At the end of the afternoon Malika and the young man, who said his name was Tex, went for a walk along the road outside the hotel, where the snow had been packed down. The peaks of the mountains around them were turning pink. She sniffed the air with enthusiasm.

I like it here, she said, as though the subject had been under discussion.

You'd like it more if you learned to ski, he told her.

No, no!

She hesitated, then went on quickly: I can't pay for lessons. I haven't any money. They don't give me any.

Who's they?

She walked on beside him without answering, and he took her arm. By the time they got back to the hotel she had agreed to let Tex pay for lessons, skis and clothes, on condition that the clothes be bought at a shop in the town and not at the hotel.

Once she had been fitted out, the lessons were begun, Tex being always present. Dinah did not like the idea at all. She said it was unheard-of, and she asked Malika to point Tex out to her.

Malika, who had felt no resentment at being left each day to her own devices, could not understand Dinah's objections. She was delighted with her new friend, and arranged for Dinah to meet him in the bar, where she sat for a half hour listening to them speak in English. Later that night Dinah told her Tex was uncivilized. Melika did not understand.

He's an idiot! Dinah cried.

Malika laughed, for she took this to mean that Dinah also liked him. He has a good heart, she replied calmly.

Yes, yes. You'll see that good heart soon enough, Dinah told her with a crooked smile.

Having observed that Tex's interest in her was due in part to the mystery with which she seemed to be surrounded, Malika offered him as little information about herself as possible. He was still under the impression that she was Mexican and a member of Dinah's family, and that for one reason or another Dinah was in charge of her. His misconception amused Malika, and she did nothing to correct it. She knew Dinah and Daphne were persuaded that she and Tex were having an affair, and this pleased her, too, since it was not true.

Sometimes, in spite of Malika's efforts to restrain him, Tex drank too much whisky. This generally happened in the bar after dinner. At such moments his face often took on an expression that made her think of a fish dragged up onto the beach. His eyes bulging, his jaw slack, he would take one of her hands in both of his, and groan: Oh, Honey! To Malika this was an expression of momentary despair. She would sigh and shake her head, and try to comfort him by saying that he would feel better in a little while.

The lessons were going very well; Malika spent most of the daylight hours on the snow with Tex. She would have eaten at his table, too, if Dinah had not indignantly forbidden it.

One day at lunch Dinah lit a cigarette and said: You're going to have your last skiing lesson tomorrow. We're leaving for Paris on Thursday.

Malika saw that she was watching her closely to observe the effect of her announcement. She decided to look slightly crestfallen, but not enough to give Dinah any satisfaction.

It's been a marvellous holiday, Dinah went on, and we've all had a fine time, but now it's over.

Así es la vida, murmured Malika with lowered head.

XII

That afternoon when the lesson was over, Malika and Tex sat side by side in the snow, looking out across the valley in the fading light. All at once she found that she was sobbing. Tex stared at her in consternation, then drew her to him, trying to comfort her. Through her sobs, she repeated what Dinah had told her at lunch.

When she felt his arms around her, she knew that the only reason for her unhappiness was that she did not want to leave him. She leaned her head on his chest and sobbed: *Me quiero quedar contigo, Tex, contigo.*

These words transformed him. He began to glow. While he soothed her with gestures, he told her he would do anything in the world for her. If she wanted him to, he would take her away that very night. She stopped weeping and listened.

Before they rose from the snowbank, they had agreed upon the following morning for their departure, while Dinah would be out skiing. Tex was determined to have no further meeting with Dinah, but Malika made him leave a note behind for her, which she dictated.

Dinah, I don't want to go to Paris now. Thank you and thank Daphne. I loved Cortina. Now I'm going to learn to ski. I'll be in Switzerland for a while. Good luck, Malika.

Tex had made arrangements to have a chauffeur-driven car large enough to hold Malika's many valises pick them up at the hotel at half past nine in the morning. Everything went off smoothly. Malika handed the note for Dinah to the receptionist. He did not mention the subject of her bill, which she had feared he might do, but merely nodded gravely.

As they left Cortina behind them, Malika said: Dinah's going to be very angry.

I'm thinking of that, said Tex. Will she make trouble?

She can't do anything. She never saw my passport. She doesn't even know my name.

Tex appeared to be stunned by this information, and began to put a whole series of questions to her, but she, being happy to see the beautiful white landscape outside, replied without answering them, seized his hand now and then to draw his attention to a detail in the landscape, and, by taking gentle command, succeeded in putting him off without his being aware of it.

They had lunch at a small restaurant in Mezzolombardo. The waiter brought a bottle of wine and poured out two glasses. No, said Malika, pushing it away.

Your friend Dinah's not here now, Tex reminded her. You can do whatever you like.

Dinah! she scoffed. What's Dinah beside the words of God?

He stared at her, mystified, without pursuing the matter further, and drank the bottle of wine by himself, so that he was in a happy and relaxed state when they got back into the car. As they rolled southward on the autostrada he devoted himself to crushing her hand in his, nuzzling her neck with his lips, and finally kissing her feverishly on the lips. Malika could not have hoped for more.

XIII

At dinner that night in Milano she watched him drink two bottles of wine. Later in the bar he had several whiskies. At Cortina she would have begged him to stop, but this night she affected not to notice that he was resolutely sliding into a drunken state. Instead, she began to tell him a complicated story she had known since her childhood, about a female ghoul that lived in a cave and unearthed newly buried corpses to extract their livers. Seeing his expression of total bewilderment, she stopped halfway through the tale.

He shook his head. What an imagination! he said.

I want to learn how to speak English, Malika went on, leaving the ghoul behind. That's what I'm going to do in Switzerland.

Tex was drunk by the time they went upstairs. She regretted this, for she liked him much better when he was sober. But she suspected that he was going to want to sleep with her and she thought it wiser for their first time together that he be in a state of befuddlement. It was imperative that he believe himself to be the first to have had her.

In the morning when he awoke staring, trying to remember, she confided that it had not been as painful as she had expected. Tex was contrite; he nearly wept as he begged her forgiveness. She smiled and covered him with kisses.

Having won this much, she pressed on, not with any specific purpose in mind, but simply to gain a stronger foothold. While he was still in the slough of early-morning remorse, she made him promise to abjure whisky.

At the Grand Saint Bernard, as the police handed back their passports, Malika saw Tex stare at hers briefly with astonishment. When they were in the car, he asked to see the passport again. The Arabic characters seemed to cause him great excitement. He began to ask her questions about Morocco which she could not have answered even if she had been in the mood for such conversation. She assured him it was like any other country. Now I'm looking at Switzerland, she said.

They arrived in Lausanne at sunset and took rooms in a large hotel by the lake, at Ouchy. It was far grander than the hospice at Cortina, and the people living there, not being dressed for skiing, seemed to Malika much more elegant.

I like it here, she said to Tex that night at dinner. How long can we stay?

The next morning, at Malika's insistence, they went together to the Berlitz School for intensive language courses: she in English and he in French. She saw that Tex imagined she would soon tire of the strict schedule, but she was determined not to leave Lausanne before she could converse in English. They spent each morning in their respective classes, had lunch together, and returned to the school at three for further tutoring.

Every Friday afternoon Tex would rent a car, and they

would drive to Gstaad, stopping to have dinner on the way. Saturdays and Sundays if no snow fell, they skied at Wasserngrat or Eggli. Sometimes he would insist on staying over until Monday, even though it meant missing their morning classes. Malika could see that if she had let him have his way he always would have done this, and very likely would have extended the weekends further and further. He approved of Malika's learning English, but he could not fathom her obsessive preoccupation with it. Nor, had he asked her, could she have explained it to him. She knew only that unless she kept on learning she was lost.

XIV

During the winter there in Lausanne they made no friends, being entirely satisfied with each other's company. One day as they were coming out of the Schweizerische Kreditanstalt, where Tex had opened an account for Malika, he turned to her and apropos of nothing asked her if she had ever thought of being married.

She looked at him wonderingly. I think of it all the time, she said. You know it makes me happy to be married to you.

He stared at her as if he had understood nothing she had said. After a moment he seized her arm and pulled her to him. It makes me happy, too, he told her. She could see, however, that something was on his mind. Later when they were alone, he said that of course it was true that they were married, but that what he had been speaking of was marriage with papers.

With papers or not with papers! It's the same thing, isn't it? If two people love each other, what have papers got to do with it?

It's the governments, he explained. They like married people to have papers.

Of course, she agreed. In Morocco, too. Many people are married with papers.

She was about to add that papers were important if you expected to produce children, but she checked herself in time, sensing that the observation bordered on dangerous ground. Already, from certain questions he had put to her, she suspected that he had begun to wonder if she were pregnant. His questions amused her, based as they were on the supposition that there had been no Tim before Tex, to show her how always to be safe.

One morning in early spring when she complained of feeling tired, he asked her outright.

You think Moroccan women don't know anything? she cried. If they want to make children they make them. If they don't, they don't make them.

He nodded dubiously. Those home remedies don't always work.

She saw that she was safe. He knew nothing about Morocco. Mine does, she said.

If she never mentioned America to him or asked about his family, it was because she could not envisage his life there with enough clarity to be curious about it. For his part, he spoke of America with increasing frequency. Never before had he stayed away for so long, he said. Malika interpreted these remarks as warnings that he had had enough of his present life and was contemplating a change. The thought struck terror to her heart, but she would not let him perceive this.

From time to time she would catch him in the act of staring at her, an expression of utter incomprehension on his face. By now, at Malika's insistence, they often spoke together in English. She thought it suited him much better than Spanish; he seemed to have an altogether different voice.

Would you like to be married? With papers, I mean.

Yes, if you want to.

And you? he insisted.

Of course I want to, if you want to.

They were married in the rectory office of a Protestant minister, who remarked in an aside to Tex that personally he was not in favour of marriage where the bride was as young as Malika. In my experience, he said, very few such unions prove to be permanent.

To Malika the episode was a bit of nonsense of the sort that Nazarenes appear so much to enjoy. Nevertheless she saw clearly that it was a matter of great importance to Tex. Indeed, his character seemed to have undergone a subtle metamorphosis since the ceremony, in that he was now more self-assertive. She liked him rather better this way, and concluded that secretly he was a very devout man. The papers were obviously a requirement of the Nazarene religion; now that he had them he felt more secure.

It was only a fortnight later that Tex, after drinking a little more wine than was his habit, announced to her that they were going home. Malika received the news with a sinking sensation. She could see that he was glad to be leaving the world of hotels and restaurants, and she suspected that life in a house would be very different and not nearly so much fun.

Once again she saw nothing from the plane, but this time the journey went on for such a long time that she grew worried. Tex was sleepy, nevertheless she disturbed him several times to ask: Where are we?

Twice he answered jovially: In the air. The next time he said: Somewhere over the ocean, I suppose. And he stole a glance at her.

We're not moving, she told him. We're standing still. The plane is stuck.

He only laughed, but in such a way that she realized she had made a mistake of some sort. I don't like this plane, she said.

Go to sleep, Tex advised her.

She shut her eyes and sat quietly, feeling that she had gone much too far away – so far that now she was nowhere. Outside the world, she whispered to herself in Arabic, and shivered.

XV

Being in Los Angeles persuaded Malika that she was right, that she had left behind everything that was comprehensible, and was now in a totally different place whose laws she could not know. They went from the airport to the top of the mountain, where a house was hidden in the woods. Tex had told her about it, but she had imagined something very different, like the Mountain in Tangier, where the villas had big gardens around them. This house was buried among the trees; she could not see the rest of it even when they went up to the door.

In the middle of the forest, she said wonderingly.

An ugly little Filipino in a white jacket opened the door for them. He bowed low and made a short formal speech of welcome to Malika. She knew he was speaking English, but it was not the English she had been taught in Lausanne. At the end she thanked him gravely.

Later she asked Tex what the little man had been saying.

He was hoping you'd be happy here in your new house, that's all.

My house? But it's your house, not mine!

Of course it's yours! You're my wife, aren't you?

Malika nodded. She knew, no matter what anyone pretended, that when men grew tired of their wives they put them out, and took new ones. She loved Tex and trusted him, but she did not expect him to be different from other men. When the time came, she knew he would find a pretext to rid himself of her. The important point was to know how to fight off the fatal moment, to make it come as late as possible. She nodded again and said with a smile: I like this house, Tex.

The rooms had irregular shapes, with unexpected alcoves and niches where there were soft couches with piles of cushions. As she inspected the house she noted with satisfaction that the windows were barred with iron grille work. She had already seen the massive front door with its heavy bolts.

That night as they sat in front of the fireplace they heard the yapping of coyotes.

Jackals, murmured Malika, turning her head to listen. Very bad.

She found it incomprehensible that anyone should waste

money building such a pretty house in a place so far from everything. Above all she could not understand why the trees had been left growing so close to the house. Silently, she determined never to go outside unless Tex accompanied her, and never under any circumstances to remain in the house without him.

The next morning, when Tex was about to drive down into the city, Malika began to run from room to room, crying: Wait! I'm going with you.

You'd be bored, he told her. I've got to go to a lawyer's office. You stay here with Salvador.

She could not let Tex know that she was afraid to stay in the house; it would be an unforgivable affront. No, no, no. I want to see the town, she said.

He kissed her and they set out for the city. It was a bigger car than the one he had rented at the airport the day before.

I always want to go with you no matter where you go, she confided, hoping that this declaration would aid in establishing a precedent.

During these weeks, when she watched the life in the streets, she could find no pattern to it. The people were always on their way somewhere else, and they were in a hurry. She knew better than to imagine that they were all alike; still, she had no way of knowing who was who. In Morocco, in Europe, there had been people who were busy doing things, and there had been others watching. Always, no matter where one was or what one was doing, there were watchers. She had the impression that in America everyone was going somewhere and no one sat watching. This disturbed her. She felt herself to be far, far away from everything she had ever known. The freeways inspired her with dread, for she could not rid herself of the idea that some unnameable catastrophe had occurred, and that the cars were full of refugees fleeing from the scene. She had ample opportunity to observe the miles of small houses set side by side, and compare these simple dwellings with the house on the mountain. As a result it occurred to her that perhaps she was fortunate to live where she did. One day as they drove into the city she turned to Tex and said: Do you have more money than these people?

What people?

She moved her hand. The ones who live in these houses.

I don't know about other people's money, he said. I know I never have enough of my own.

She looked out at the rows of frail wooden houses with their dusty shrubbery, and could not believe him. You *do* have more money, she declared. Why don't you want to say it?

This made him laugh. Whatever I have, I made myself. The day I was twenty-one my father handed me a cheque and said: Let's see what you can do with this. In three years I changed it into four and a half times as much. Is that what you meant, Dad? I asked him. That's what I meant, son, he said.

Malika thought a moment, saying finally: And now when he needs money you give it to him.

Tex looked sideways at her and said gravely: Of course.

She wanted to ask him if he had no friends in Los Angeles. Since their arrival she had not met anyone, and she thought this strange. It could be a custom here for recently married couples to keep strictly to themselves during a specified period. Or perhaps Tex's friends here were all girls, which would automatically preclude her knowing them. When she asked him, he said he seldom came to Los Angeles. I'm generally with my family in Texas, he said, or down at the hacienda.

There was a studio upstairs with a wide sun-deck that was not hidden by trees in the middle of the day. Malika did not feel entirely at ease sitting out there, with nothing between her and the dark forest. She suspected that the trees harboured dangerous birds. Sometimes she and Tex sat up here between dips in the pool, which, being below inside the closed patio, she considered safe. Tex would observe her as she lay stretched on a mattress, and assure her she was more beautiful than ever. She had noticed this herself, but she was pleased to know that he too had seen it.

XVI

One day Tex told her that a man named F. T. was coming to dinner. F. T. was an old friend of his father's, who managed his financial affairs for him. Malika was interested to hear what such work entailed, so Tex made an effort to explain the mechanics of investment. She was quiet for a while. But then you can't make money unless you already have it, she said.

That's about it, Tex agreed.

F. T. was middle-aged and well-dressed, with a small grey moustache. He was delighted with Malika, and called her Little Lady. This struck her as vaguely insulting, but since she could see that he was a pleasant and well-behaved man otherwise, she made no objections. Besides, Tex had told her: Remember. If you should ever need anything, anything at all, just call F. T.'s number. He's like my father.

During dinner she decided that she really liked F. T., even though he seemed not to take her very seriously. Afterward he and Tex talked together for a long time. The words went on for so long that Malika fell asleep on a divan and awoke only after F. T. had gone. She was apologetic for having been rude, but she blamed Tex for allowing it to happen.

He threw himself down beside her. F. T. thought you were great. He says you're beyond a doubt the most beautiful girl he's ever seen.

He's a nice man, she murmured.

Ever since her arrival in California, her life had seemed static. When she thought back about it, she decided that it had stopped moving when she had left the Berlitz School. Innocently, she asked Tex if she might continue the lessons here. To her astonishment he ridiculed the suggestion, claiming that all she needed was practice in conversation. Because he was not in the habit of refusing her anything, she did not take him at his word, and continued to dwell on her desire for further instruction. All at once she saw that he was going to be firm; he seemed to consider her dissatisfaction a criticism of him. Finally she realized that he was angry.

You don't understand! she cried. I have to study English more before I can study anything else.

Study!

Of course, she said calmly. I'm always going to study. You think I want to stay like this?

I hope you do, Honey, for my sake. You're perfect.

He took hold of her, but she wriggled free.

That evening Tex said to her: I'm going to get an extra woman in the kitchen and let Salvador give you lessons in cooking. That's something you should learn, don't you think?

Malika was silent. Do you want me to learn? You know I want to make you happy.

She began to spend several hours each day in the kitchen with Salvador and Concha, a Mexican girl of whose work the little Filipino was scornful. It was a pleasant enough room, but the number of strange machines and the little bells that kept sounding as Salvador rushed from one spot to another awed and confused her. She was even a bit afraid of Salvador, because his face never changed its fixed expression – that of a meaningless grin. It seemed to her that when he was annoyed the grin became even wider. She took care to pay strict attention to everything he told her. Soon he had her making simple dishes which they ate at lunch. If the recipe called for a béchamel or a chasseur, he made it himself and incorporated it, since the timing was more than Malika could manage. It gratified her to see that Tex thought her food good enough to be served at table. She continued to spend two hours in the kitchen each morning, and another hour or so before dinner in the evening. Sometimes she helped Salvador and Concha prepare a picnic hamper, and they went to the beach. She would have liked to tell Tex about the picnics on the beach at Tangier, but there was no way of doing that.

XVII

Occasionally, despite Malika's entreaties, Tex would take

advantage of her morning session in the kitchen to drive the small car into the city on an errand. She would be uneasy until he returned, but he was always back in time for lunch. One morning he failed to appear at the usual hour. The telephone rang. Salvador wiped his hands and stepped into the butler's pantry to answer it, while Malika and Concha went on chatting together in Spanish. In a moment Salvador reappeared in the doorway, and with a radiant smile told Malika the police had called to say that Mister Tex had met with an accident and was in a hospital in Westwood.

Malika rushed at the little man and seized him by the shoulders. Telephone to F. T.!

She hopped up and down while he searched for the number and dialled it. As soon as she saw that he was speaking to F. T., she snatched the telephone from his hand.

F. T.! Come and get me! I want to see Tex.

She heard F. T.'s voice, calm and reassuring. Yes. Now you just wait quietly for me. I'll be there as soon as I can. Don't you worry. Let me speak to Salvador again.

She left Salvador talking into the telephone and rushed upstairs to the studio, where she began to walk back and forth. If Tex was in hospital, he probably would not be home to sleep that night, and she would not stay in the house without him. She went out onto the sun-deck and stared at the trees. Tex is dead, she thought.

It was mid-afternoon before F. T.'s car drew up at the door. He found her in the studio lying face down on a couch. When she heard his voice she sprang up, wide-eyed, and ran to him.

That night Malika slept at F. T.'s house. He had insisted upon taking her home with him and leaving her in the care of his wife. For it was true that Tex was dead; he had succumbed not long after reaching the hospital.

F. T. and his wife did not commiserate with Malika. Mrs F. T. said a show of sympathy could induce hysteria. Malika merely talked on and on, weeping intermittently. Sometimes she forgot that her listeners did not know Arabic or Spanish, until at their prompting she would go back into English. She had sworn to accompany Tex whenever he went out, and she had not done so, therefore he had been killed, he was the only being in the world she loved, and she was far from home, and what was going to become of her here alone?

That night as she lay in the dark listening to the occasional passing wail of a police siren, she was assailed afresh by the sensation she had felt on the plane – that of having gone too far for the possibility of return. Being with Tex had made it possible to accept the strangeness of the place; now she saw herself as someone shipwrecked on an unknown shore peopled by creatures whose intentions were unfathomable. And no one could come to rescue her, for no one knew she was there.

She slept at F. T.'s house for several nights. During the days she visited supermarkets and other points of interest with Mrs F. T. You've got to keep busy, her hostess told her. We can't have you brooding.

There was no way, however, of preventing Malika from worrying about what was to become of her, stranded in this unlikely land without a peseta to buy herself bread, and only the caprice of F. T. and his wife between her and starvation.

XVIII

One morning F. T. himself drove Malika to his office. Out of respect for him she had dressed with great care in a severe grey silk suit from Balenciaga. Her entrance into the office with F. T. caused a stir of interest. When she sat facing him across his desk in a small inner room, he pulled a sheaf of papers from a drawer. As he leafed through them he began to talk.

Betty tells me you're worried about money.

Seeing Malika nod, he went on. I take it you haven't any at all. Is that right?

She felt in her handbag and pulled out a crumpled twenty-dollar bill that Tex had given her one day when they were shopping.

Only this, she said, showing him.

F. T. cleared his throat.

Well, I want you to stop worrying. As soon as we get everything cleared up you'll have a regular income. In the meantime I've opened a checking account for you at the bank downstairs in this building.

He saw anxiety flitting across her face, and added hastily: It's your money. You're his sole beneficiary. After taxes and all the rest, you'll still have a substantial capital. And if you're wise you'll leave it all just where it is, in certificates of deposit and treasury notes. So stop worrying.

Yes, she said, understanding nothing.

I never let Tex play with stocks, F. T. went on. He had no head for business.

She was shocked to hear F. T. denigrate poor Tex in this way, but she said: I see.

When we get everything straight and running smoothly, you ought to have around fifty thousand a month. Possibly a little more.

Malika stared at F. T. Is that enough? she asked cautiously.

He shot a quick glance at her over his spectacles. I think you'll find it's enough.

I hope so, she said with fervour. You see, I don't understand money. I never bought anything myself. How much does a thing cost? I don't know. Only in my own country.

Of course. F. T. pushed a cheque book along the top of the desk toward her. You understand, this is a temporary account for you to draw on now, until all the legal work is finished. I hope you won't overdraw. But I'm sure you won't.

He smiled encouragingly at her. Remember, he went on. There are only twenty-five thousand dollars there. So be a good girl and keep track of your cheques.

But I can't do what you tell me! she exclaimed. Please do it for me.

F. T. sighed. Can you write your name? he asked very quietly.

Tex showed me in Lausanne, but I've forgotten.

In spite of himself, F. T. raised his arms. But my dear lady, how do you expect to live? You can't go on this way.

No, she said miserably.

F.T. pushed back his chair and stood up. Well, he said jovially, what you don't know you can always learn. Why don't you come up here every morning and study with Miss Galper? She's as smart as a whip. She'll teach you everything you need to know. That's my suggestion for you.

He was not prepared for her vehement response. She jumped up and hugged him. Oh, F.T.! That's what I want! That's what I want!

XIX

The following day Malika moved her luggage into a hotel in Beverly Hills. Under F.T.'s advice she kept Salvador on, living in the house, but now functioning solely as chauffeur. Each morning he called at the hotel for her and drove her to F.T.'s office. She found this routine stimulating. Miss Galper, a pleasant young woman with glasses, would spend the forenoon working with her, after which they generally went to lunch together. There had not been much glamour in Miss Galper's life, and she was fascinated by Malika's accounts of Europe and Morocco. There remained a basic mystery in her story, nevertheless, since she never explained how she came to be living at Tim's flat in Tangier. In her version, she might have come into being during a picnic on the beach at Sidi Qacem.

When after two months F.T. saw that Malika was, if anything, even more serious and determined about pursuing her practical education, he suggested that the lessons continue at the hotel. Now it was Miss Galper whom Salvador drove to and from Beverly Hills. Occasionally they went shopping - small expeditions to Westwood that delighted Malika because for the first time she was aware of prices, and could gauge the buying power of her money. F.T. had told her that with what Tex had left for her she would be able to live better than most people. At the time she had supposed this was a part of his attempt to comfort her, but now that she understood the prices she realized that he had been stating a fact. She said nothing to Miss Galper of her surprise at finding the cost of goods so low. Instead, she overwhelmed her with a constant flow of small gifts.

You've got to stop this, Malika, Miss Galper told her.

The first month they had done nothing but arithmetic. After that there was the telling of time, the names of the days and the months. With some difficulty Miss Galper taught her to sign the two forms of her name: *Malika Hapgood* and *Mrs Charles G. Hapgood*. By the time the lessons were moved to the hotel, Malika had begun to practise writing out in words complicated sums given her in figures. They went back to dates, and she had to learn to write them correctly.

You can leave everything else to a secretary, Miss Galper told her. But you've got to take care of your money yourself.

To this end she gave Malika a course in reading bank statements, and another in spacing the purchase of securities to assure regular turnover.

As the months went by and Malika's insight into the functioning of the world around her grew, she began to understand the true extent of her ignorance, and she conceived a passionate desire to be able to read the texts of newspapers and magazines.

I'm not an English teacher, Miss Galper told her. F. T. doesn't pay me for that. We can get you a good professor whenever you want.

Malika, being persuaded that she could learn only from Miss Galper, consulted F. T. about it. After a certain amount of deliberation, he devised a plan which delighted Malika and pleased Miss Galper as well. He would give Miss Galper a year's holiday with salary if Malika wanted to take her on as a paid companion during that time. In this way, he implied to Malika, she would be able to get the reading lessons she wanted. He added that he did not think Miss Galper was the person to give them, but since Malika had her heart set on being taught by her, this seemed to him a viable strategy.

It was Miss Galper's idea to make a tour of Europe. F. T. suggested they buy a big car, put it on a freighter, and take Salvador along with them to pick it up over there and drive it. When Malika heard this, she asked why they could not all go on the ship with the car. It might be possible, F. T. told her.

Eventually F. T. had arranged to get Malika a new passport, had even helped Miss Galper and Salvador expedite theirs, and, accompanied by Mrs F. T., had bidden them a lengthy farewell at the dock in San Pedro. It was a comfortable Norwegian freighter bound for Panama and eventually for Europe.

The ship was already in tropical waters. Malika said she had imagined it could be this hot only in the Sahara, and certainly not on the sea. She had nothing to do all day. Salvador spent most of his time sleeping. Miss Galper sat in a deck chair reading. She had refused to give Malika any kind of lessons while they were on the ship. It would make me seasick, she assured her. But she noticed Malika's boredom, and talked with her for long periods of time.

XX

Malika could not sit, as Miss Galper could, looking at the sea. The flat horizon on all sides gave her much the same sensation of unreality she had experienced on the plane with Tex. Panama came as a relief, making it clear that the ship had not been static during all those days, and that they had reached a very different part of the world.

It took all day to go through the canal. Malika stood on deck in the sun, waving back to the men working along the locks. But from Panama on, her restlessness increased daily. She was reduced to playing endless games of checkers with a yawning Salvador each afternoon in the narrow passengers' lounge. They never spoke during these sessions. From the beginning of the voyage the captain had urged Malika to visit the bridge. At some point Miss Galper had mentioned that he had the power to seize anyone on the ship and have him locked into a dark cell somewhere below. When Malika finally accepted his invitation she took Miss Galper along.

Standing at the prow, Malika stared ahead at the white buildings of Cadiz. As the ship moved into the port, the combination of the light in the air, the colour of the walls and the odours on the wind told her that she was back in her part of the world and close to home. For a long time she had refused to think about the little house above the gully. Now that it no longer frightened her, she was able to imagine it almost with affection.

It was her duty to go and visit her mother, however hostile a reception she might get from her. She would try to give her money, which she was certain she would refuse to take. But Malika was ready with a ruse. If her mother spurned the money, she would tell her she was leaving it next door with Mina Glagga. Once Malika was out of the way, her mother would lose no time in going to claim it.

Miss Galper had hoped to spend the night in Cadiz, but Malika insisted on driving straight to Algeciras. Now that she was so near home, she wanted to get there as soon as she could. I must see my mother, she said. I must see her first.

Of course, said Miss Galper. But you haven't seen her in two years or more and she isn't expecting you. One day sooner or later?

We can come back. Now I have to go and see my mother.

In Algeciras at the hotel that night they saw Salvador eating at the other end of the long dining room. He had changed from his uniform into a grey flannel suit. Malika observed him carefully, and said: He's drinking wine.

He'll be all right tomorrow, Miss Galper told her. They always drink, Filipinos.

He was at the door grinning when they came out of the hotel in the morning to be driven to the dock. Most of the passengers going to Tangier were Moroccans. Malika had forgotten the shameless intensity with which her countrymen stare at women. Now she was back among her own kind. The realization startled her; she felt both excitement and apprehension.

XXI

After they had settled into their quarters at the hotel, Malika went down to the desk. She hoped to visit her mother in the evening, when she was sure to be in the house, and when there would be a valid excuse for not staying too long. She intended to reserve two rooms in Tetuan for the night, one for Salvador and one for herself, and return to Tangier in the morning. In the lobby they told her of a new hotel on the beach only a mile or so from her town. She asked them to telephone for reservations.

Miss Galper's room was down the corridor from hers. Malika knocked on her door and told her she would be leaving about five o'clock, in order to get to the hotel before dark.

Miss Galper looked at her searchingly. I'm glad you're doing it now and getting it over with, she said.

You can have a good time, Malika told her. There are bars where you can go.

No, thank you. The men here give me the creeps. They all try to talk to you.

Malika shrugged. What difference does it make? You can't understand what they're saying.

This was fortunate, she thought. The brutally obscene remarks made by the men to women passing in the street disgusted and infuriated her. Miss Galper was lucky not to know any Arabic.

She said a lame good-bye and hurried to her room. The prospect of seeing her mother had unsettled her. Mechanically she put a few articles of clothing into an overnight bag. On the way out she cashed some traveller's cheques at the office, and soon she and Salvador were on the road to Tetuan.

The mountains had scarves of white cloud trailing outward from their summits. Salvador criticized the narrow highway. Malika scarcely heard his complaints. Her heart was beating unusually fast. It was true that she was going back to help her mother; she was going because it was included in the pattern. Since the day she had run away, the vision of the triumphant return had been with her, when she would be the living proof that her mother had been mistaken, that she was not like the other girls of the town. Now that the moment was drawing near, she suspected that the visit was foredoomed to failure. Her mother would feel no pleasure at seeing her – only rancour and bitterness at the thought that she had been with Nazarenes.

Salvador said: In Pilipinas we got better roads than this one.

Don't go fast, she told him.

They skirted Tetuan and turned to the left along the road that led to her town. The sea wind rushed through the car. *Bismil'lah*, she murmured under her breath, for now she was entering the crucial part of the journey.

She did not even know they had reached the town until they were in the main street. It looked completely different. There were big new buildings and bright lights. The idea that the town might change during her absence had not occurred to her; she herself would change, but the town would remain an unmoving backdrop which would help her define and measure her transformation.

A moment later they had arrived at the new hotel, spread out along the beach in a glare of green floodlights.

XXII

Malika soon discovered that it was not a real hotel. There was no room service, and in the dining room they served only snack-bar food. Before eating, she changed into blue jeans, bought in Los Angeles at Miss Galper's suggestion. She wore a sweater and wrapped a silk kerchief tightly around her head. In this costume she felt wholly anonymous.

Salvador was already eating at the counter in the comedor. She sat on a stool near him and ordered pinchitos. Her stomach rebelled at the thought of eating, but she chewed and swallowed the meat because she had learned that to feel well she must eat regularly. Through the rasping of a transistor radio at the end of the counter she heard the dull, repeated sound of the waves breaking over the sand below. If her mother flew into a rage and began to beat her, she would go directly to Mina Glagga and give her the money, and that would finish it. She signed the chit and went out into the wind to the car.

The town's new aspect confused her. They had moved the market; she could not see it anywhere, and she felt a wave of indignation at this betrayal. Salvador parked the car at the service station and they set out on foot up the narrow street that led to the house. There were street lights only part of the way; beyond, it would have been dark had it not been for the moon. Salvador glanced ahead and said it would be better to turn around and come again in the morning.

You wait here, she said firmly. I'll come back as soon as I can. I know the way. And she quickly went on, before he could argue about it.

She made her way up along the empty moonlit street until she came to a small open square from which, in the daytime at least, her mother's house was visible ahead, at the edge of the barranca. Now as she looked, the moon's light did not seem to strike it at all; she could see no sign of it. She hurried on, already assailed by a nightmarish premonition, and then she stopped, her mouth open in disbelief. The house was not there. Even the land where it had stood was gone. Mina Glagga's and all the houses bordering on the gully had disappeared. Bulldozers had made a new landscape of emptiness, a great embankment of earth, ashes and refuse that stretched downward to the bottom of the ravine. The little house with its garden had been just below where she now stood. She felt her throat tighten painfully as she told herself that it no longer existed.

Ceasing finally to stare at the meaningless terrain, she turned and went back to the square, where she knocked at the door of one of the houses. The woman who opened the door was a friend of her mother's whose name she had forgotten. She eyed Malika's blue jeans with distaste and did not ask her inside. They talked standing in the doorway. In an expressionless voice the woman told her that her mother had died more than a year earlier, during Ramadan. It was fortunate, she added, that she had not lived to see them destroy her house in order to build the new road. She thought Malika's sister had gone to Casablanca, but she was not certain.

By now the woman had pushed the door so that it was nearly shut. Malika thanked her and said good-night.

She went over and stood at the edge of the landfill, staring down at the uniform surface of the hillside, unreal even in the careful light dropped over it by the moon. She had to force her eyes shut to clear them of the tears that kept forming, and she found it strange, for she had not felt tenderness for her mother. Then she saw more clearly. It was not for her mother that she felt like weeping; it was for herself. There was no longer any reason to do anything.

She let her gaze wander over the dim expanse toward the mountains beyond. It would be good to perish here in the place where she had lived, to be buried along with the house under the hateful mass. She pounded the edge of it with her heel, lost her footing, and slid downward some distance through mounds of ashes and decayed food. In that instant she was certain it was happening, as a punishment for having wished to be dead a moment ago; her weight had started a landslide that would roll her to the bottom, leaving her under tons of refuse. Terrified, she lay still, listening. There were faint stirrings and clinks around her, but they quickly died away into silence. She scrambled up to the roadbed.

A cloud had begun to move across the moon. She hurried down the hill toward the street light where Salvador waited.

Allal

He was born in the hotel where his mother worked. The hotel had only three dark rooms which gave on a courtyard behind the bar. Beyond was another smaller patio with many doors. This was where the servants lived, and where Allal spent his childhood.

The Greek who owned the hotel had sent Allal's mother away. He was indignant because she, a girl of fourteen, had dared to give birth while she was working for him. She would not say who the father was, and it angered him to reflect that he himself had not taken advantage of the situation while he had had the chance. He gave the girl three months' wages and told her to go home to Marrakesh. Since the cook and his wife liked the girl and offered to let her live with them for a while, he agreed that she might stay on until the baby was big enough to travel. She remained in the back patio for a few months with the cook and his wife, and then one day she disappeared, leaving the baby behind. No one heard of her again.

As soon as Allal was old enough to carry things, they set him to work. It was not long before he could fetch a pail of water from the well behind the hotel. The cook and his wife were childless, so that he played alone.

When he was somewhat older he began to wander over the empty table-land outside. There was nothing else up here but the barracks, and they were enclosed by a high blind wall of red adobe. Everything else was below in the valley: the town, the gardens, and the river winding southward among the thousands of palm trees. He could sit on a point or rock far above and look down at the people walking in the alleys of the town. It was only later that he visited the place and saw what the inhabitants were like. Because he had been left behind by his mother they called him a son of sin, and laughed when they looked at him. It seemed to him that in this way they hoped to make him into a shadow, in order not to have to think of him as real and alive. He awaited with dread the time when he would have to go each morning to the town and work. For the moment he helped in the kitchen and served the officers from the barracks, along with the few motorists who passed through the region. He got small tips in the restaurant, and free food and lodging in a cell of the servants' quarters, but the Greek gave him no wages. Eventually he reached an age when this situation seemed shameful, and he went of his own accord to the town below and began to work, along with other boys of his age, helping to make the mud bricks people used for building their houses.

Living in the town was much as he had imagined it would be. For two years he stayed in a room behind a blacksmith's shop, leading a life without quarrels, and saving whatever money he did not have to spend to keep himself alive. Far from making any friends during this time, he formed a thorough hatred for the people of the town, who never allowed him to forget that he was a son of sin, and therefore not like others, but *meskhot* – damned. Then he found a small house, not much more than a hut, in the palm groves outside the town. The rent was low and no one lived nearby. He went to live there, where the only sound was the wind in the trees, and avoided the people of the town when he could.

One hot summer evening shortly after sunset he was walking under the arcades that faced the town's main square. A few paces ahead of him an old man in a white turban was trying to shift a heavy sack from one shoulder to the other. Suddenly it fell to the ground and Allal stared as two long dark forms flowed out of it and disappeared into the shadows. The old man pounced upon the sack and fastened the top of it, at the same time beginning to shout: Look out for the snakes! Help me find my snakes!

Many people turned quickly around and walked back the way they had come. Others stood at some distance, watching. A few called to the old man: Find your snakes fast and get them out of here! Why are they here? We don't want snakes in this town!

Hopping up and down in his anxiety, the old man turned to Allal. Watch this for me a minute, my son. He pointed at the sack lying on the earth at his feet, and snatching up a basket he had been carrying, went swiftly around the corner into an alley. Allal stood where he was. No one passed by.

It was not long before the old man returned, panting with triumph. When the onlookers in the square saw him again, they began to call out, this time to Allal: Show that berrani the way out of the town! He has no right to carry those things in here. Out! Out!

Allal picked up the big sack and said to the old man: Come on.

They left the square and went through the alleys until they were at the edge of town. The old man looked up then, saw the palm trees black against the fading sky ahead, and turned to the boy beside him.

Come on, said Allal again, and he went to the left along the rough path that led to his house. The old man stood perplexed.

You can stay with me tonight, Allal told him.

And these? he said, pointing first at the sack and then at the basket. They have to be with me.

Allal grinned. They can come.

When they were sitting in the house Allal looked at the sack and the basket. I'm not like the rest of them here, he said.

It made him feel good to hear the words being spoken. He made a contemptuous gesture. Afraid to walk through the square because of a snake. You saw them.

The old man scratched his chin. Snakes are like people, he said. You have to get to know them. Then you can be their friends.

Allal hesitated before he asked: Do you ever let them out?

Always, the old man said with energy. It's bad for them to

be inside like this. They've got to be healthy when they get to Taroudant, or the man there won't buy them.

He began a long story about his life as a hunter of snakes, explaining that each year he made a voyage to Taroudant to see a man who bought them for the Aissaoua snake-charmers in Marrakesh. Allal made tea while he listened, and brought out a bowl of kif paste to eat with the tea. Later, when they were sitting comfortably in the midst of the pipe-smoke, the old man chuckled. Allal turned to look at him.

Shall I let them out?

Fine!

But you must sit still and keep quiet. Move the lamp nearer.

He untied the sack, shook it a bit, and returned to where he had been sitting. Then in silence Allal watched the long bodies move cautiously out into the light. Among the cobras were others with markings so delicate and perfect that they seemed to have been designed and painted by an artist. One reddish-gold serpent, which coiled itself lazily in the middle of the floor, he found particularly beautiful. As he stared at it, he felt a great desire to own it and have it always with him.

The old man was talking. I've spent my whole life with snakes, he said. I could tell you some things about them. Did you know that if you give them majoun you can make them do what you want, and without saying a word? I swear by Allah!

Allal's face assumed a doubtful air. He did not question the truth of the other's statement, but rather the likelihood of his being able to put the knowledge to use. For it was at that moment that the idea of actually taking the snake first came into his head. He was thinking that whatever he was to do must be done quickly, for the old man would be leaving in the morning. Suddenly he felt a great impatience.

Put them away so I can cook dinner, he whispered. Then he sat admiring the ease with which the old man picked up each one by its head and slipped it into the sack. Once again he dropped two of the snakes into the basket, and one of these, Allal noted, was the red one. He imagined he could see the shining of its scales through the lid of the basket.

As he set to work preparing the meal Allal tried to think of other things. Then, since the snake remained in his mind in spite of everything, he began to devise a way of getting it. While he squatted over the fire in a corner, he mixed some kif paste in a bowl of milk and set it aside.

The old man continued to talk. That was good luck, getting the two snakes back like that, in the middle of the town. You can never be sure what people are going to do when they find out you're carrying snakes. Once in El Kelaa they took all of them and killed them, one after the other, in front of me. A year's work. I had to go back home and start all over again.

Even as they ate, Allal saw that his guest was growing sleepy. How will things happen? he wondered. There was no way of knowing beforehand precisely what he was going to do, and the prospect of having to handle the snake worried him. It could kill me, he thought.

Once they had eaten, drunk tea and smoked a few pipes of kif, the old man lay back on the floor and said he was going to sleep. Allal sprang up. In here! he told him, and led him to his own mat in an alcove. The old man lay down and swiftly fell asleep.

Several times during the next half hour Allal went to the alcove and peered in, but neither the body in its burnous nor the head in its turban had stirred.

First he got out his blanket, and after tying three of its corners together, spread it on the floor with the fourth corner facing the basket. Then he set the bowl of milk and kif paste on the blanket. As he loosened the strap from the cover of the basket the old man coughed. Allal stood immobile, waiting to hear the cracked voice speak. A small breeze had sprung up, making the palm branches rasp one against the other, but there was no further sound from the alcove. He crept to the far side of the room and squatted by the wall, his gaze fixed on the basket.

Several times he thought he saw the cover move slightly, but each time he decided he had been mistaken. Then he caught his breath. The shadow along the base of the basket was moving.

One of the creatures had crept out from the far side. It waited for a while before continuing into the light, but when it did, Allal breathed a prayer of thanks. It was the red and gold one.

When finally it decided to go to the bowl, it made a complete tour around the edge, looking in from all sides, before lowering its head toward the milk. Allal watched, fearful that the foreign flavour of the kif paste might repel it. The snake remained there without moving.

He waited a half hour or more. The snake stayed where it was, its head in the bowl. From time to time Allal glanced at the basket, to be certain that the second snake was still in it. The breeze went on, rubbing the palm branches together. When he decided it was time, he rose slowly, and keeping an eye on the basket where apparently the other snake still slept, he reached over and gathered together the three tied corners of the blanket. Then he lifted the fourth corner, so that both the snake and the bowl slid to the bottom of the improvised sack. The snake moved slightly, but he did not think it was angry. He knew exactly where he would hide it: between some rocks in the dry river bed.

Holding the blanket in front of him he opened the door and stepped out under the stars. It was not far up the road, to a group of high palms, and then to the left down into the oued. There was a space between the boulders where the bundle would be invisible. He pushed it in with care, and hurried back to the house. The old man was asleep.

There was no way of being sure that the other snake was still in the basket, so Allal picked up his burnous and went outside. He shut the door and lay down on the ground to sleep.

Before the sun was in the sky the old man was awake, lying in the alcove coughing. Allal jumped up, went inside, and began to make a fire in the mijmah. A minute later he heard the other exclaim: They're loose again! Out of the basket! Stay where you are and I'll find them.

It was not long before the old man grunted with satisfaction. I have the black one! he cried. Allal did not look up from the corner where he crouched, and the old man came over, waving a cobra. Now I've got to find the other one.

He put the snake away and continued to search. When the fire was blazing, Allal turned and said: Do you want me to help you look for it?

No, no! Stay where you are.

Allal boiled the water and made the tea, and still the old man was crawling on his knees, lifting boxes and pushing sacks. His turban had slipped off and his face ran with sweat.

Come and have tea, Allal told him.

The old man did not seem to have heard him at first. Then he rose and went into the alcove, where he rewound his turban. When he came out he sat down with Allal, and they had breakfast.

Snakes are very clever, the old man said. They can get into places that don't exist. I've moved everything in this house.

After they had finished eating, they went outside and looked for the snake between the close-growing trunks of the palms near the house. When the old man was convinced that it was gone, he went sadly back in.

That was a good snake, he said at last. And now I'm going to Taroudant.

They said good-bye, and the old man took his sack and basket and started up the road toward the highway.

All day long as he worked, Allal thought of the snake, but it was not until sunset that he was able to go to the rocks in the oued and pull out the blanket. He carried it back to the house in a high state of excitement.

Before he untied the blanket, he filled a wide dish with milk and kif paste, and set it on the floor. He ate three spoonfuls of the paste himself and sat back to watch, drumming on the low wooden tea-table with his fingers. Everything happened just as he had hoped. The snake came slowly out of the blanket, and very soon had found the dish and was drinking the milk. As long as it drank he kept drumming; when it had finished and raised its head to look at him, he stopped, and it crawled back inside the blanket.

Later that evening he put down more milk, and drummed again on the table. After a time the snake's head appeared, and finally all of it, and the entire pattern of action was repeated.

That night and every night thereafter, Allal sat with the snake, while with infinite patience he sought to make it his friend. He never attempted to touch it, but soon he was able to summon it, keep it in front of him for as long as he pleased, merely by tapping on the table, and dismiss it at will. For the first week or so he used the kif paste; then he tried the routine without it. In the end the results were the same. After that he fed it only milk and eggs.

Then one evening as his friend lay gracefully coiled in front of him, he began to think of the old man, and formed an idea that put all other things out of his mind. There had not been any kif paste in the house for several weeks, and he decided to make some. He bought the ingredients the following day and after work he prepared the paste. When it was done, he mixed a large amount of it in a bowl with milk and set it down for the snake. Then he himself ate four spoonfuls, washing them down with tea.

He quickly undressed, and moving the table so that he could reach it, stretched out naked on a mat near the door. This time he continued to tap on the table, even after the snake had finished drinking the milk. It lay still, observing him, as if it were in doubt that the familiar drumming came from the brown body in front of it.

Seeing that even after a long time it remained where it was, staring at him with its stony yellow eyes, Allal began to say to it over and over: Come here. He knew it could not hear his voice, but he believed it could feel his mind as he urged it. You can make them do what you want, without saying a word, the old man had told him.

Although the snake did not move, he went on repeating his command, for by now he knew it was going to come. And after another long wait, all at once it lowered its head and began to move toward him. It reached his hip and slid along his leg. Then it climbed up his leg and lay for a time across his chest. Its body was heavy and tepid, its scales wonderfully smooth. After a time it came to rest, coiled in the space between his head and his shoulder.

By this time the kif paste had completely taken over Allal's mind. He lay in a state of pure delight, feeling the snake's head against his own, without a thought save that he and the snake were together. The patterns forming and melting behind his eyelids seemed to be the same ones that covered the snake's back. Now and then in a huge frenzied movement they all swirled up and shattered into fragments which swiftly became one great yellow eye, split through the middle by the narrow vertical pupil that pulsed with his own heartbeat. Then the eye would recede, through shifting shadow and sunlight, until only the designs of the scales were left, swarming with renewed insistence as they merged and separated. At last the eye returned, so huge this time that it had no edge around it, its pupil dilated to form an aperture almost wide enough for him to enter. As he stared at the blackness within, he understood that he was being slowly propelled toward the opening. He put out his hands to touch the polished surface of the eye on each side, and as he did this he felt the pull from within. He slid through the crack and was swallowed by darkness.

On awakening Allal felt that he had returned from somewhere far away. He opened his eyes and saw, very close to him, what looked like the flank of an enormous beast covered with coarse stiff hair. There was a repeated vibration in the air, like distant thunder curling around the edges of the sky. He sighed, or imagined that he did, for his breath made no sound. Then he shifted his head a bit, to try to see beyond the mass of hairs beside him. Next he saw the ear, and he knew he was looking at his own head from the outside. He had not expected this; he had hoped only that his friend would come in and share his mind with him. But it did not strike him as being at all strange; he merely said to himself that now he was seeing through the eyes of the snake, rather than through his own.

Now he understood why the serpent had been so wary of him: from here the boy was a monstrous creature, with all the bristles on his head and his breathing that vibrated inside him like a far-off storm.

He uncoiled himself and glided across the floor to the alcove. There was a break in the mud wall wide enough to let him out. When he had pushed himself through, he lay full length on the ground in the crystalline moonlight, staring at the strangeness of the landscape, where shadows were not shadows.

He crawled around the side of the house and started up the road toward the town, rejoicing in a sense of freedom different from any he had ever imagined. There was no feeling of having a body, for he was perfectly contained in the skin that covered him. It was beautiful to caress the earth with the length of his belly as he moved along the silent road, smelling the sharp veins of wormwood in the wind. When the voice of the muezzin floated out over the countryside from the mosque, he could not hear it, or know that within the hour the night would end.

On catching sight of a man ahead, he left the road and hid behind a rock until the danger had passed. But then as he approached the town there began to be more people, so that he let himself down into the seguia, the deep ditch that went along beside the road. Here the stones and clumps of dead plants impeded his progress. He was still struggling along the floor of the seguia, pushing himself around the rocks and through the dry tangles of matted stalks left by the water, when dawn began to break.

The coming of daylight made him anxious and unhappy. He clambered up the bank of the seguia and raised his head to examine the road. A man walking past saw him, stood quite still, and then turned and ran back. Allal did not wait; he wanted now to get home as fast as possible.

Once he felt the thud of a stone as it struck the ground somewhere behind him. Quickly he threw himself over the edge of the seguia and rolled squirming down the bank. He knew the terrain here: where the road crossed the oued, there were two culverts not far apart. A man stood at some distance ahead of him with a shovel, peering down into the seguia. Allal kept moving, aware that he would reach the first culvert before the man could get to him.

The floor of the tunnel under the road was ribbed with hard little waves of sand. The smell of the mountains was in the air that moved through. There were places in here where he could have hidden, but he kept moving, and soon reached the other end. Then he continued to the second culvert and went under the road in the other direction, emerging once again into the seguia. Behind him several men had gathered at the entrance to the first culvert. One of them was on his knees, his head and shoulders inside the opening.

He now set out for the house in a straight line across the open ground, keeping his eye on the clump of palms beside it. The sun had just come up, and the stones began to cast long bluish shadows. All at once a small boy appeared from behind some nearby palms, saw him, and opened his eyes and mouth wide with fear. He was so close that Allal went straight to him and bit him in the leg. The boy ran wildly toward the group of men in the seguia.

Allal hurried on to the house, looking back only as he reached the hole between the mud bricks. Several men were running among the trees toward him. Swiftly he glided through into the alcove. The brown body still lay near the door. But there was no time, and Allal needed time to get back to it, to lie close to its head and say: Come here.

As he stared out into the room at the body, there was a great pounding on the door. The boy was on his feet at the first blow, as if a spring had been released, and Allal saw with despair the expression of total terror in his face, and the eyes with no mind to them. The boy stood panting, his fists clenched. The door opened and some of the men peered inside. Then with a roar the boy lowered his head and rushed through the doorway. One of the men reached out to seize him, but lost his balance and fell. An instant later all of them turned and began to run through the palm grove after the naked figure.

Even when, from time to time, they lost sight of him, they could hear the screams, and then they would see him, between the palm trunks, still running. Finally he stumbled and fell face downward. It was then that they caught him, bound him, covered his nakedness, and took him away, to be sent one day soon to the hospital at Berrechid.

That afternoon the same group of men came to the house to carry out the search they had meant to make earlier. Allal lay in the alcove, dozing. When he awoke, they were already inside. He turned and crept to the hole. He saw the man waiting out there, a club in his hand.

The rage always had been in his heart; now it burst forth. As if his body were a whip, he sprang out into the room. The men nearest him were on their hands and knees, and Allal had the joy of pushing his fangs into two of them before a third severed his head with an axe.

The Husband

Abdallah lived with his wife in a two-room house on a hillside several miles from the centre of town. They had two children. The girl was in school and the boy lived at the house of an Englishman for whom he did gardening.

Long ago the woman had set the pattern of their life by going out to work as a maid in Nazarene houses. She was strong and jolly, and the Nazarenes liked her. They recommended her to their friends, so that she was never without employment, and was able to work at several houses each day. Since she turned over all her wages to Abdallah, there was no need for him to work. Sometimes he suspected that the Nazarenes were paying her more than she claimed, but he said nothing.

The woman was also expert at carrying things out of the houses of the Nazarenes without their being aware of it. In earlier days she had handed over these bits of plunder to him along with the money; what they brought at the joteya was a welcome bonus. Working so long for the Nazarenes, however, had given her a taste for the way the Nazarenes lived. She began to complain when Abdallah tried to carry off a bath towel or a sheet or a fancy serving dish, for she wanted these things in the house with her. When he took away a small travelling alarm clock which she particularly prized, she stopped speaking to him and would have nothing to do with him. He was angry and mortified, and he began to sleep in the other room, sending the girl to sleep with her mother.

The silent war between them had not gone on for very long before Abdallah took a great interest in Zohra, a young woman living up the road, whose husband only recently had left her. Because she needed money, she encouraged Abdallah's attentions, and soon he was eating and sleeping in her house with her, not caring that his behaviour was causing unfavourable comment throughout the neighbourhood.

Zohra was not long in discovering that Abdallah could not pay for anything. Having moved out of his house, he could scarcely go back at the end of the month and ask his wife for money. Once she saw how matters stood, Zohra thought only of getting rid of him, and she did her utmost to make his life unbearable.

Early one afternoon he paid a visit to his house, knowing that his wife would be away at work. It was a Friday, so that his daughter was not at school. She was in the patio, washing out some clothes. He greeted her, but she scarcely looked up. Her mother has filled her head with lies about me, he thought. Then he went inside and called his wife's name. At the same time his eye alighted on a transparent plastic bag, stuffed into a niche in the wall. He stepped nearer and saw something shining inside the bag. Without looking further, he hid it inside his djellaba, called his wife's name once more, and returned to the patio.

Tell your mother I was here, he said to the girl. She did not reply, and he added: Don't listen to the neighbours.

She fixed him for a second with a resentful stare before she bent again to scrub the clothes.

He climbed up the hillside and sat down in the woods so he could examine the contents of the bag in private. There were twelve big spoons there, all of them exactly alike. After admiring them for a while, he wrapped them up and set out for the town to show them to a friend in Emsallah who knew about such things.

The man assured him that the soup spoons were of the purest silver, and offered to give him seventy thousand francs for them. Abdallah said he needed time to consider it, and that he would return. From Emsallah he went directly to the joteya and put the silver in the hands of a dillal, who began to make the rounds of the market with it. The bids finally reached a hundred thousand francs and the spoons were sold.

That night at Zohra's he lay awake, fully dressed, with the banknotes clutched in his hand. Early in the morning he went out and bought ten goats, all of them black. Then he rented a shack with a shed beside it where he could keep them at night. He was careful to choose a quarter that lay at some distance from his own, one that was reached by a different road, reasoning that this would reduce the likelihood of an unexpected encounter with Zohra or his wife.

He found his new life agreeably restful. Each morning at daybreak he went out with the goats, driving them along the back road to Boubana and then through the valley toward Rehreh. Here he would sit in the shade of a ruined farmhouse and look down at the goats as they wandered over the hillside.

Sometimes he fell asleep for a while as he sat watching them. This was dangerous: they could get into a patch of cultivated ground and he would have trouble with the farmer. Even more important was a recently passed law stipulating that henceforth no motorist would be held responsible for any livestock he happened to hit on the highway. Worse than that, it was the owner of the animals who had to pay a stiff fine for each one killed. The country people were unable to fathom the reasons for an order that seemed so perverse, but they understood that it was wiser to keep their animals far from the road.

Often when the weather was hot Abdallah did not take the trouble to drive the goats up the valley, but sat under a pine tree in a field not far from the road to Rmilat. Here he was obliged to force himself to stay awake and keep his eye on them, for they could easily stray onto the road. One breathless afternoon, however, he felt a powerful need for sleep overtaking him, and even though he fought against it, he was unable to keep from dropping into a deep slumber.

He awoke to a squealing of brakes, looked down at the road, and saw what had happened. Two of his goats had wandered in front of a truck, and lay dead on the asphalt.

He jumped up, drove the others away from the road, and

then hurried back to drag the two dead animals over to the ditch. If the police were to pass by now, they would immediately identify them as part of his flock, and take him with them.

A youth whom he recognized as the son of the man who lived next door to his shack came along, pushing an empty wheelbarrow. He called to him, and pointed to the bodies in the ditch.

Get rid of these for me, will you? I don't care where you hide them, but don't go along the road with them. When you come back here with the empty wheelbarrow you get the money.

He did not explain to the boy why he was so eager to remove the carcasses instead of simply leaving them there in the ditch for the dogs. If the boy realized the importance of his task, he would be dissatisfied with the small amount Abdallah intended to give him.

The lad heaved the two goats into the wheelbarrow and set off along a path that led through the scrub down toward the river. It was a Sunday, and scores of women were doing their washing along the banks of the stream; the bushes were tents of drying sheets. He pushed the wheelbarrow along until he came to the bridge over the sluice. On the upper side the water was deep and black; on the other side a rivulet trickled at the bottom of a twisting gully. He decided to dump the goats into the deep water, and rolled up his sleeves.

At that moment a woman standing on the bank at the foot of the bridge began to shout at him. It was her land he was standing on, she cried, and he could take his carrion somewhere else. He let her shout and watched her wave her arms for a long time, saying nothing. Then, seeing that a crowd was gathering, he spat contemptuously, tipped the wheelbarrow and let the animals splash into the water. The woman's voice rose to a scream as she announced that she was going to the police.

I know you! she shrieked. I know where your father lives! You'll sleep in jail!

The boy did not even look at her as he pushed his wheelbarrow ahead of him. To get to where Abdallah was waiting for him, he went along the highway.

When Abdallah saw him coming, he walked to meet him, noted the empty wheelbarrow, and paid him, assuming that the goats were hidden somewhere among the bushes and brambles near the bend in the river.

Less than an hour later the woman was at the comisaría waving her arms as she denounced the boy. The police listened attentively, feeling certain that they were on their way to collecting some fines.

When they had fished the goats out of the water and dumped them in a back room at the police station, the woman led them to the house of the boy's father.

The boy was indignant. Deep water's the best place to throw them, he protested. The man paid me to take them away. Ask him.

On the adjoining plot of land they found Abdallah sitting dejectedly with his eight remaining goats. Come on, they said. We've got something to show you. And they made him go with them to the comisaría, where they confronted him with the two wet carcasses, and demanded an immediate payment of forty thousand francs.

Abdallah was shocked. I haven't even got ten, he said.

That's all right, they told him. We'll take four of your goats.

At this Abdallah set up an outcry. How can two goats be worth four? he kept shouting. They laughed and pushed him out, but the scene had been so noisy that people had gathered outside the entrance, trying to see in through the front door. Zohra, who was waiting for a bus on the other side of the road, quickly got the story from others who stood nearby.

Ah, so he has goats, she said to herself, and as she rode up the hill in the bus all her rancour against Abdallah returned. He could never even pay for a loaf of bread, but he has goats.

She set about spreading the news around the neighbourhood that Abdallah, contrary to what everyone thought, had not left

Tangier at all, but lived below Vasco da Gama with a flock of goats. She was certain that this would get to Abdallah's wife, which it very soon did.

Abdallah's wife had never bothered to file a complaint against him for having abandoned her and the children, since she knew she would get nothing out of it. Now however she determined to go and claim support. If Abdallah had goats, he had them only because of her spoons; of that she was certain. He must not be allowed to keep them.

The following day, instead of reporting to work at the Nazarenes', she went to declare that her husband had left her. After a long wait, she was allowed into an office. As he filled out a paper, the official asked her where Abdallah worked.

He doesn't work. He has no money.

The man raised his arms. Then what do you expect us to do? If he has no money, why did you come here?

He has goats, she said.

A few weeks later a message from the government arrived for her, telling her to go to the comisaría of her quarter. There a policeman was assigned to her, and together they started to walk to the shack where Abdallah lived.

Ever since the police had gone away with half his flock, Abdallah had not taken the trouble to drive the four remaining goats out to the fields where they could graze. He merely sat in the doorway of his shack, watching the starving animals wander around the small enclosure. Once in a while he brought in an armful of weeds for them.

The policeman told the woman to wait in the road while he went in and got the goats. She peered through the gate and saw the four bony, dried-up creatures. The policeman was talking, and then he came out through the gate, driving the goats ahead of him.

As he shut the gate she stole another glance inside and saw Abdallah sitting by the door of the shack, his face buried in his hands. At that moment, if only he had looked up, she would have called out something to him, to make him understand that it was all right, that he could return to her. But he did not move.

The gate cut across her view of him, and she was in the road, walking with the policeman and the goats.

For an instant she regretted not having spoken to him: he looked so solitary and hopeless. Then she remembered the shawl. Three days earlier, after months of planning, she had managed to avail herself of a huge soft cashmere shawl which she intended to keep. She thought she had done well to hold her tongue.

In this world it's not possible to have everything, she told herself.

Reminders of Bouselham

When I was a boy, Mother's favourite spot for reading, the place where she sat when she was going to read for a long time, was an old chaise longue, kept always in the same position in a corner of the east room, far enough from the walls so that the light came in over her shoulders on both sides. The back of the chaise longue was piled with dozens of small down-stuffed cushions. It was a comfortable seat to recline in. Sometimes I would use it for a few minutes in the morning before she was up. Once she caught me there and ridiculed me.

Getting decrepit in your old age! she scoffed. You're a growing boy. That's a chair for an adult.

The garden was the place to lie on a summer afternoon. Overhead the wind hissed in the high eucalyptus and cypress trees. There were flying skeins of fog that swept by very fast, just above, sometimes catching the tops of the trees and swooping down through the branches. One summer when I was back from school in England I did all my studying out there on the ground behind bushes or hedges, or anywhere that was hidden from the sight of the house.

And I would lie face-down in the hot garden, and look beneath the cut tips of the grass spears, into the miniature forest where the ants lived. Most of them were very small, and were not troubled by the mat I spread out over their domain. If the large red ones discovered it, as now and then they did, they attacked at once, and there was nothing to do but carry the mat somewhere else.

It went without saying that the Medina was forbidden

territory. Mother would have reacted very badly had she known I had ever been in it alone. But from time to time I went on an errand and had the opportunity to slip into the old town and find my way along the alleys for a few minutes. I loved the way they suddenly changed direction and burrowed under the houses. In fact, you went under a house to get into the alley where Mama Tiemponada's brothel stood. Hers was not the only one there, but it was the biggest. All the houses in the alley were brothels. The women leaned in the doorways and made remarks to the men walking by. I found the place mysterious and sinister. It seemed natural enough that Mother should not want me to come to the Medina.

One evening as I stood outside Mama Tiemponada's in the alley watching the door, it opened and a single Moroccan boy came out. He stood still for an instant, and looking up at the full moon directly above, whistled once at it, then walked away. This struck me as very strange, and I remembered it. The whistle was casual and intimate, suggesting that the moon and he had been good friends for a long time. A year or two later, when Bouselham came to work for us, I thought I recognized him as the same boy.

Probably it would have been better for me if I'd got to know Father, but I never did. It did not occur to me to wonder what sort of man he was. His fiftieth birthday was well behind him when I was born, and by then he was interested primarily in golf. He paid no attention to me, and very little to Mother. At daybreak he would get up, eat a big breakfast, and ride his favourite horse to the country club at Boubana. We would not see him again until evening. The ladies said to Mother: Colonel Driscoll is so impressive up there on his horse! Their own husbands drove in their cars to the country club. I was convinced that they were secretly laughing at us because Father was so odd.

As a boy I sometimes played with Amy, because she lived on the property next to ours, down the road. She was five years older than I, a tomboy, and full of sadistic impulses which she often vented on me. When she was twenty her mother died, and Amy was left alone in a house far too big for her. Then she began to spend almost all her time with Mother.

I was not surprised when Mother announced casually one day: Amy has a buyer for Villa Vireval. She's coming to stay with us for a while.

Soon Amy was with us. She had changed with the years, and was now an introverted, nervous young woman with a passion for precision. She had an annoying tic: the constantly repeated clearing of her throat. In the beginning Father made an effort to converse with her, even though he was very much against having her with us. She was neurotic, he said; she was morbid and self-centred, and she sapped Mother's energy.

What's wrong with that girl? Can't she leave you alone for a minute?

Mother, who like anyone else enjoyed being admired, was grateful even for Amy's devotion.

She's a well-balanced girl. I can't think what you have against her.

As usual the gossip got the basic facts fairly straight, but the motivations wrong. Everyone was certain that Father had left home because of Bouselham, when actually it was because he could no longer bear to be in the same house with Amy. He put up with her for six months. Then, seeing that she had no intention of leaving, and that Mother was adamant in her refusal to suggest to her that she find another place to live, he suddenly went off to Italy. Mother was unperturbed. Your father needs a holiday, she said to me after he had gone. Of course she assumed he would return.

It was precisely at that point that Bouselham emerged from his obscurity. Father had engaged him a year or so earlier, when he was sixteen, as an assistant gardener. He weeded, raked, and carried water in the lower garden, and one seldom saw him anywhere near the house. But when Father left, he began to come into the kitchen, where the maids would give him tea. Before long he was eating regularly there with them, rather than sitting under a tree with whatever he had brought with him from home.

How did the relationship start between him and Mother? What was the beginning of it? There is no way of bringing up the subject with Bouselham, since it has never been mentioned and thus does not exist between us. But I know that whatever the beginning may have been, it was Mother who set it in motion.

Often Bouselham had nothing to do but sit in a café smoking kif, and it was not always certain that there would be someone who could play cards with him. Most men worked during the day and came into the café after they had finished. Bouselham did not have to work. Ever since the colonel had gone away he had been with the colonel's wife. She did not want him to work, because then he would have to get up very early every morning, whereas she liked to sleep late and have him with her. All the men in the café knew that Bouselham had a rich Nazarene woman who gave him whatever he wanted.

And this was what Amy eventually began to say to Mother in one way or another, over and over. In her view it was wrong of Mother to have Bouselham with her, not only because his culture, religion and social class were not hers, but also because he was too young for a woman of her age. Usually Mother replied blandly that she didn't agree, but now and then she said a bit more. I heard her say one day: You're trying to encroach on my private life, Amy, and you have no right to.

Not too long after that, Amy decided to go to Paris where a friend had invited her. She packed up very quickly and was suddenly gone. Mother limited her comment to saying: Amy's a very sweet girl who has everything to learn, I'm afraid. And whether she will or not, I wonder.

The day Amy left I wandered into her room and looked around. It needed a thorough cleaning. I pulled the bureau out from the wall and peered down behind it. Underneath, wedged behind a back leg, was a crumpled postcard-size glossy print of Bouselham in bathing trunks on the beach at Sidi Qanqouch. For me this put Amy's quarrel with Mother in a new light. For a moment I was even sorry she was gone; it would have been fun to see what a few leading questions might have brought out from behind those thin precise lips of hers. Had she coveted Bouselham for herself? Or did Mother interrupt something that was already going on between them when she brought Bouselham into the house to sleep in her room?

The tale had been going around Tangier for many months. I heard it first from an English woman; she had just arrived here, and so had no way of knowing that the subject of her story was my mother. The colonel's wife used to disappear every night into the dark corners of the garden to meet the gardener, who was no more than a boy, an ordinary Moroccan workman. And when the colonel had had enough of her nonsense he had left, whereupon she had calmly taken the servant into the house and lived with him. I'm told she's even given him a racing car! she added, pretending to burst into laughter.

Probably, I said.

There is no doubt that Mother changed in certain respects during the time Bouselham was living in the house. She did buy a second-hand Porsche convertible for him, and this was certainly most unlike her. Her manner became distant; she seemed uninvolved in all the things that heretofore had been her life. When I suggested that I move out of the house and take a flat in town, she merely raised her eyebrows. You'll come to dinner twice a week, was all she said.

What finally decided her against Bouselham was a long and complicated saga involving his sister. Once she had carefully checked the details of the story, her resolve to get rid of him was instantaneous. However, the only way she could devise for accomplishing this was so drastic as to be laughable. Mother has lived in this country for many years, and should not have been so deeply disturbed by Bouselham's behaviour, particularly since it had nothing whatever to do with her. To me what he did seems natural enough, but then, I was born here. I first heard about it from Bouselham himself, not long after I moved out of the house and took the apartment in town.

I had been out to dinner and had walked home afterward. A thunderstorm was approaching from the direction of the strait. Soon hail showered against the windows. There was a very bright bolt of lightning, and the electricity was gone. I got out a flashlight, started some candles burning, and stood in front of the fireplace for a while. The thunderstorm circled around and came back, and it rained harder. In the midst of this there was a banging on the door, and when I opened it I found Bouselham standing there, completely wet.

He looked as wild and as pleased with himself as ever, in spite of the rivulets of rain running down his face. Immediately he took off his shoes and socks and crouched in front of the fireplace, almost inside it, while he talked. Every day, he said, he was seeing a lawyer friend of his who was helping him.

To do what? I asked.

Avoiding a direct answer, he pivoted on his heels to face me, and asked if I could let him have ten thousand francs. The lawyer had to have the money for photocopies and notarizations. His fee would be contingent upon the success of his case, later. As soon as I had agreed to let him have the money, the story began to come out.

A certain rich merchant of the Medina, intent on the pleasures of the twilight hour, used to go each day and sit in a café at the end of the city. Here he could see in three directions, and hundreds of people were visible nearby and in the distance, walking along the roads. Each day, sooner or later, a girl passed by with an older woman who carried a basket. He sat at a table on the sidewalk, facing in the direction from which they always came, so that he could see them from far away, and watch the girl as she approached. Every afternoon he saw her eyes pick him out from among the others at the café, but from that moment on she would give no sign of knowing he was there.

How many years since I've seen such a beauty? he sighed. He would notice them coming far down the road under the eucalyptus trees, long before she could see him, for they were walking into the sunset light. The instant came when she saw him, and then her head bent forward. The rich merchant would watch her as she came nearer, his eyes never leaving her. It seemed to him that she was dancing rather than walking, and as she went past, often so near that he could have touched her djellaba by stretching out his arm, he was exasperated by the impossibility of speaking with her.

Maybe one day they'll let her out by herself, he thought, and so he waited.

The day finally came when he saw her walking along carrying the basket herself, and no one was with her. Ah, he said softly, rubbing the ends of his fingers together. He called the waiter and paid him. Then he sat quietly until she had gone by. As the girl turned the corner he got up and began to walk after her.

He caught up with her only after she had gone into another street. May I drive you somewhere? he asked her.

You may drive me home if you like, she said.

This was not what the rich merchant had hoped to hear. However, he led her to his car, which was parked not far away.

I brought Bouselham a cup of coffee. He sipped it, still crouching by the fire, and said nothing for several minutes. Then abandoning his story-telling manner, he went on casually, as though recapitulating a tale I already knew.

And I was just coming out of a bacal there, and I saw this Mercedes parked up ahead. And not with Belgian licence-plates, either. Moroccan ones, and that means money. And then, while I was still looking, I stopped believing what I was seeing, because the door of the car opened and my sister got out and ran up toward the corner. I knew she'd seen me and didn't think I'd seen her. The first thing I thought of was going after her and killing her. While I stood there the car drove away. I didn't see the man or get the number.

What good would that have done, if you'd killed her? I said, although I knew that for him it was one of those meaningless European remarks. Surprisingly, he laughed and said: I'm not that stupid. I felt sorry for her, though, that night when I got her alone at home and saw how frightened she was.

I saw you get out of the car, I told her. But then I said: You say he's always at the Café Dakhla. Tomorrow you're going to show me which one he is. As you walk past him you're going to cough.

And she did, and when he left the café I followed him and saw him get into his Mercedes. I watched him drive away and I thought: Maybe. Maybe. Incha'Allah!

Once he had identified the man though his licence-plate, he began to ask questions, first going to the qahouaji there in the café, and then having narrowed his search, to several merchants and bazaar-keepers in the city.

I found out more about him than his mother knows, said Bouselham. He owns half the textile factory at the Plaza Mozart, and an apartment house in the Boulevard de Paris. And three bazaars. So one night when I got home, I took my sister up on the roof where we could talk, and I said to her: You like this Qasri?

She began to stammer and protest. I don't even know him. How can I say if I like him?

That made me angry and I grabbed her. You don't know whether you like him. But you got into his car and sat beside him. What does that mean?

She thought I was going to hit her, and she hid her face in her hands and backed away. I had the right to beat her, of course. But I let her know I was on her side, and would never mention it to the rest of the family. I even bought her new clothes the next day, so El Qasri could get some idea of how she could look if she wanted to. And I decided to wait and see if things happened by themselves.

He kept after her and she went on putting him off. Then once my father and mother and the whole family had to go to Meknes overnight, and she and I were the only ones who stayed home. I thought: I'm going to spend the night in Tetuan and see what happens. So I told her I wasn't going to be there that night, and that she would have to sleep at our aunt's house. And I asked her please not to mention my trip to Tetuan to our parents, because of course I was supposed to be in the house taking care of her. I thought: If anything's going to happen by itself, tonight's the night when it'll happen. And I was right. I went to Tetuan and she went with him to his house, and it wasn't a long time later when she came to me and said she thought there was a child in her belly.

Right away I took her over to Gibraltar, to the biggest hospital. We stayed there four days, and I got the papers on each test, and there was no doubt about it, they said: there was a child inside.

Having nothing more urgent to do with his time, Bouselham continued to go each day to the café at the end of the city. Here he fell into conversation and eventual companionship with the rich merchant. Even after he had brought his sister back from Gibraltar, and the lawyer was busy preparing his strategy, even after the lawyer had called on the rich merchant to advise him that the only way of avoiding a scandal was to ask for the girl in marriage, before her family discovered her pregnancy, Bouselham sat daily with him in the café listening to the story of his troubled romance.

She's got a brother, the rich merchant told him. He's the one who wants my blood. The son of a whore found out about it.

Then Bouselham said to him: But why son of a whore? He's letting you marry her. If he wanted to, he could put you in jail today. Are you crazy? She was a virgin.

The rich merchant agreed that this was so. Less than a week later he made the offer of marriage to Bouselham's father.

After he stopped talking, I looked down at him, trying to see the expression on his face, but his head was outlined against the flames, and there was only the light of two candles in the room.

He's not going to like it much when he finds out you're her brother, I said.

He only laughed. Some day, he said. Some day.

I brought a fresh log, and he finally stood up.

Bouselham did not keep silent about the dubious part he'd played in the arranging of his sister's wedding; on the contrary, he discussed it at length with his Moroccan friends. To him it was a business matter in whose success he took a healthy pride. Thus several garbled versions of the story began to travel around Tangier. Mother heard them, but discounted them as fables invented purely out of spite. It was not until months after Bouselham's visit to me at the flat that she brought herself to accepting them as fact. At that instant she became irrational.

The whole thing is vile! she said. I've got rid of him. His dismissal had been summary, with no explanation offered. She had handed him a sum of money and told him to leave the premises instantly. Two days later she had set out for Italy. It was clear to me that she half expected to be blackmailed, but was ashamed to put it into words. If only she had mentioned her fear, I could have tried to reassure her. I believe I know Bouselham better than she did. Until the day when he called to me from inside the Café Raqassa, I had not seen him for several weeks. We sat in a back corner where it was dark and the air smelled of damp cement and charcoal smoke. Bouselham spoke briefly of Mother, shaking his head ruefully. There was no mention of anything more than that he had lost his job as gardener when Madame went away. He was aware of somehow having offended her, but her arbitrary behaviour had bewildered and aggrieved him. The way he saw it, he had been turned out of the house for no reason at all. Still, as we parted, he said: When you write to Madame, tell her Bouselham sends his greetings.

I did not pass on the message, or any subsequent ones, from him to Mother. She sold the house without returning to Tangier, and it seemed to me that living over there in Italy with Father she must be miserable enough without getting reminders of Bouselham from me.

Afternoon With Antaeus

You wanted to see me? They told you right. That's my name. Ntiuz. The African Giant's what they've called me ever since I started fighting. What can I do for you? Have you seen the town? It isn't such a bad place. You're lucky the wind's not blowing these days. We have a bad wind that comes through here. But without it the sun's too hot. Argos? Never heard of it. I've never been over to the other side.

A man named Erakli? Yes, yes, he was here. It was a long time ago. I remember him. We even put on a fight together.

Killed me! Is that what he told them back there? I see. And when you got here you heard I was still around, and so you wanted to meet me? I understand.

Why don't we sit here? There's a spring in the courtyard that has the coldest water in town. You asked about Erakli. No, he had no trouble here, except losing his fight. Why would anyone bother him? A man alone. You never saw him before. You let him go on his way. You don't bother him. Only savages attack a stranger walking alone. They kill him and fight over his loincloth. We let people go through without a word. They come in on one side and go out on the other. That's the way we like it. Peaceful and friendly with everyone. We have a saying: Never hit a man unless you know you can kill him, and then kill him fast. Up where I come from we're rougher than they are down here on the coast. We have a harder life, but we're healthier. Look at me, and I could almost be your father. If I'd lived down here on the coast all my life I wouldn't be like this now. And still I'm nothing to what I was twenty years ago. In those days I went to every festival and put on shows for the people. I'd lift a bull with one hand and hit him between the horns with the other, so he'd fall dead. People like to see that. Sometimes I broke beams with my head. That was popular, too, but the bull was religious, of course, so it was the one people wanted to see most. There was nobody who didn't know about me.

Have some nuts? I eat them all day. I get them up in the forest. There are trees up there bigger than any you ever saw.

It was at least twenty years ago he came through here, but I remember him, all right. Not because he was any good as a fighter, but because he was so crazy. You can't help remembering a man as crazy as Erakli.

Have some more. I've got a whole sack full. That's true, the flavour's not quite like anything else. I don't suppose you have them over on the other side.

I'll be only too glad to take you up to the forest, if you'd like to see it. It's not far. You don't mind climbing a little?

Of course he didn't make any friends here, but a man like that can't have friends. He was so full of great ideas about himself that he didn't even see us. He thought we were all savages, ready to swallow his stories. Even before the fight everybody was laughing at him. Strong, yes, but not a good fighter. An awful boaster and a terrible liar. And ignorant.

We'll turn here and go up this path. He talked all the time. If you believed him, there was nothing he couldn't do, and do it better than anybody else.

You'll get a fine view on the way. The edge of the world. How does it feel, when you're used to being in the middle, to be out here at the end? It must be a different feeling.

Erakli came into town without anyone noticing him. He must have had a little money with him, because he began to meet two or three men I knew every day and pay for their drinks. They told me about him, and I went along one day just to see what he looked like, not to meet him. Right away I knew he was no good. No good as a fighter, no good as a man. I didn't even take him seriously enough to challenge him. How can you take a man seriously when he has a beard that looks like the wool on a sheep?

He stayed around town a while and saw me kill a few bulls. I fought a match or two, too, while he was here, and it seems he came each time to watch me. The next thing I knew, he'd challenged me. It was he who wanted the match. It was hard to believe. And what's more, they told me he held it against me that I hadn't been the one who challenged him. It just never entered my mind.

All this land you see up here is mine. This and the forest up ahead. I keep everybody out. I like to walk, and I don't want to meet people while I'm walking. It makes me nervous. I used to fight every man I met. At least, in the beginning.

When I was a small boy in my village I liked to go late in the afternoon to a big rock. I'd sit on it and look down the valley and pretend enemies were coming. I'd let them get to a certain point, and then I'd start a boulder rolling down the mountain to hit them. I killed them every time. My father caught me and I got punished. I might have hit sheep or goats, or even men down there.

But I'm not dead, as you can see, no matter what Erakli may be saying. I want you to look at my trees. Look at the size of the trunk of that one. Follow it up, up, up, to where the first branches begin. Have you ever seen trees this big anywhere?

When I got a little older I learned how to throw a calf, and later a bull. By that time I was fighting. Never lost yet. They forgot my name was Ntiuz and began to call me The Giant. Not because of my size, of course. I'm not so big. But because nobody could beat me in a match. They came from all around, and afterwards from far away. You know how they do when they hear of a fighter who's never lost. They can't believe that somehow or other they won't manage to get him down. That was the way with your Erakli. I didn't meet him until the fight, but I'd heard all about him from my friends. He told them he'd studied me, and he knew how to beat me. He didn't say how he was going to do it. And I never even found out what he thought he was going to do until after the fight.

No, I'm not dead. I'm still the champion. Anybody here can tell you. It's too bad you never met Erakli yourself. You wouldn't be so surprised. You'd understand that whatever he said when he got back home was what he wanted to tell and nothing more. He couldn't tell the truth if he wanted to.

Are you tired? It's a steep climb if you're not used to it. The fight itself? It didn't last long. He was so busy trying to use the system he'd worked out. He'd back away, and then come up to me and just stand there with his hands on me. I couldn't understand what he was trying to do. The crowd was jeering. For a minute I thought: He's the kind that gets his pleasure this way, running his hands over a man's chest and squeezing his waist. He didn't like it because I laughed and shouted to the crowd. He was very serious the whole time. And I was wrong anyway. Are we going too fast? And you're carrying that heavy pouch at your waist. We can go as slowly as you want to. There's no hurry.

That's a good idea. Why don't we sit a minute and rest? Do you feel all right? No. Nothing. I thought you looked a little pale. It may be the light. The sun never gets down in here.

It was only after the fight that one of my friends told me what Erakli wanted to do. Instead of trying to throw me, the crazy fool was trying to lift me off the ground and hold me in the air! Not so he could throw me down better, but just to hold me up there. It's hard to believe, isn't it? But that's what he had in his mind. That was his great system. Why? Don't ask me. I'm an African. I don't know what goes on in the heads of the men of your country.

Have some more nuts. No, no, they couldn't have hurt you. It's the air. Our climate doesn't suit people from the other side. While he was trying to make up his mind how to lift me I finished him. They had to drag him out.

Shall we go on? Or would you rather wait a while? Are you still out of breath? There's no air here in the forest.

Don't you think we ought to wait a while? Of course, if you want to go. We can walk slowly. Let me help you up. It's too bad we couldn't have gone further. The biggest trees are up that way.

Yes, they dragged him out, and he stayed three days lying on a mat before he left here. Finally he limped out of town like a dog, with everybody laughing at him along the way. Hang on to me. I won't let you fall. You're walking all right. Just keep going. He didn't look left or right on his way out of town. Must have been glad to get into the mountains.

Relax. First one foot, then the other foot. I don't know where he went. I'm afraid there's no water here. We'll get some as soon as we get to town. You'll be all right. I suppose he went back where he came from. We never saw him again here, in any case.

Does it seem like such a long time that we've been walking? It's only a few minutes. You recognize the path but you don't know where you are? Why should you know where you are? It's not your forest. Relax. Step. Step. Step.

You're right. It's the rock where we were sitting a few minutes ago. I wondered if you'd notice. Of course I know my way! I thought you'd better rest again before we started into town. That's right, you just lie back there. You'll be fine as soon as you've had a little sleep. It's very quiet here.

No, you haven't been asleep so long. How do you feel now? Good. I knew a little sleep would do it. You're not used to the air here. A pouch? I don't think you were carrying anything.

There's no need to make a face like that. You don't think I took it, do you?

I thought we were friends. I treated you like a friend. And now you pay me back.

I'm not going to take you anywhere. Get down to the town by yourself. I'm going the other way.

Go on back to your country and tell them about me. You can walk all right.

Just keep going.

And get out of the forest fast!

Madame and Ahmed

Unless it was raining very hard, Mrs Pritchard spent roughly half of each day working outdoors in the garden. It was a garden to be admired, but not a place where one could sit. Her house was at the top of a cliff overlooking the sea; the winds sweeping through the Strait of Gibraltar struck the spot first, and blew harder there. If Ahmed thought of Madame in the garden, he saw her with her skirt fluttering in the wind and her hand over her hair, trying vainly to keep it in place.

The land sloped off at a moderate angle for a few hundred feet before the sheer drop, and the terraced garden followed it down to the end. On some levels there were long tiled pools full of goldfish; others were bounded by arbours sheltering small fountains whose water dribbled from the mouths of marble fish into basins.

She had planted the land in such a way that the flowers were superb throughout the year, thus transforming the bleak and forbidding strip of land, and she took pride in the result. Recently, however, certain large shrubs she had imported from England seemed to be doing very poorly, and since they were within sight of the house, she was upset by their sickly aspect. If guests peered out of a window she would beg them not to look, saying sadly: I'm ashamed of my garden this year.

Her friends commiserated with her, most of them advising her to find a new gardener. This worried her, for she shrank from the idea of getting rid of Ahmed. He had kept her garden in order for the past eleven years. In that time, she wondered

how many hundreds of hours she had spent squatting beside
him as, working together with trowels and clippers, they discussed the ways of plants. She felt that they knew and understood
one another in a basic and important fashion, even though
Ahmed never had learned even to pronounce her name. For
him she was Madame.

One day she came to him in excitement and said she had just
bought a large number of beautiful plants from a man in the
city who would bring them in a truck tomorrow and, she
added, help her plant them. Seeing Ahmed's expression of hurt
surprise, she explained to him that this service was included in
the price of the plants. The cost, she confessed, had been
extremely high, and she saw no reason not to take advantage of
the man's offer to assist in the work. Ahmed was unable to
follow her logic; he understood only that she was allowing an
outsider to come in and work in the garden. Yes, Madame, he
said; no more.

The following morning a stout man in a grey business suit
appeared with Madame at the top of the garden. They talked
and occasionally pointed. Ahmed, squatting on a terrace some
distance below, stared up at the man and recognized him as the
chief gardener for the municipality. A little later, returning
from a trip to the toolshed, he was able to pass near enough to
the new plants to recognize them as having come from the
Jardin Municipal. For a moment he was impelled to go and tell
Madame that she had bought stolen goods, but then he thought
better of it. During the years of working for her he had
observed that if one Moroccan spoke ill of another Moroccan
to her, she automatically took the side of the accused rather
than that of the complainer. When the time came, he might
make use of what he knew about the plants.

A second man was carrying in more pots from the truck
outside, setting them down in rows on the top terrace.
Madame was saying to the stout man: Now these will go here
along the wall, and those there in that circular bed, and I think
the tuberoses should go all the way down at the end of this
path by themselves.

I know the best place for each plant, Madame, the fat man
told her. You'll see.

Wait! she cried nervously, glancing around as if for help. I'll
send my gardener up.

The man rejected this suggestion. No, no! My assistant and I
will do everything. Each plant will be in the right place. You
leave it to me.

Mrs Pritchard seemed to wilt. She turned and went inside
the house.

The thief had taken command of the garden, not even
allowing Madame to have her plants where she wanted them.
From the lower terrace where he knelt, Ahmed watched the
two men. They were putting the plants in hurriedly, paying
little heed to what they were doing. When they had finished,
they began to walk back and forth along the two topmost
terraces, examining the flowers. He tried to hear what they
were saying, but they spoke too low. On seeing their
prolonged stop beside the giant hibiscus Madame had brought
from Hawaii, he suspected that the fat man would find a
pretext for returning to see Madame.

After the truck had driven away, Madame came out of the
house and called to Ahmed. Together they surveyed the hasty
workmanship. Madame laughed. It doesn't matter. We can
replant them later. Give them plenty of water.

He glanced at the row of agapanthus without interest. When
she mentioned the price she had paid for them, he was
indignant. You could have bought bulbs, he said reproachfully.

But I wouldn't have had the flowers until next year.

He nodded gloomily.

That evening Johara, the black cook, stopped him as he passed
the kitchen door. Do you know what he was telling Madame,
that man? He told her you weren't a real gardener, and she
should get rid of you and let him work here.

He's a criminal! Ahmed shouted.

In the shack where he lived behind the greenhouse, Ahmed
sat and thought. He must save his job, and he must save the

garden. Again he recalled the visitors' scrutiny of the hibiscus bushes. If they came there to work they would methodically strip the garden of its most valuable plants.

Once he had convinced himself that he was acting partially in Madame's interest, he felt less guilt about what he was planning to do. It was simple enough. He waited until long after all the lights in the main house had been put out. Then, taking up a sack into which he dropped a sharp knife, he stole out into the garden, to the end of the topmost terrace, and knelt down among the newly interred plants. One after the other he yanked them up, severed their roots or tubers with a swift stroke of the blade, and carefully replanted them exactly where they had been. The sack was full of roots and bulbs when he took it back to his room. He built a fire in his mijmah and charred them beyond recognition before carrying them out and scattering them over the compost heap. Then he went to bed.

In the morning Madame was out looking at the new plants. They're very pretty, she said to Ahmed. Each one needs to be watered with a sprinkling can, and before the sun hits them. Just sprinkle a little around each stalk so it can soak in.

She watched for a while as Ahmed, in resentful silence, carried out her instructions. Then, apparently satisfied, she went inside. It was many years since she had stood over him like that, waiting to see if he did as he was told, and he understood that the fat man's poison was working in her, that in spite of his open indifference to her wishes she had not rejected the idea of hiring him to run her garden.

By mid-afternoon, some of the flowers were not looking as crisp as they had looked in the morning. Ahmed noted their state as he passed by them, and decided to put off reporting it until evening, when the sun would have carried its destructive work still further.

It was Madame herself who first remarked on the poor complexions of the transplants. She called to Ahmed, who came up from the bottom of the garden.

I don't know, she said, shaking her head. As she pulled at a leaf of one of the plants, it fell over, a dry stick exposing its rootless base. She seized the next plant and lifted it up.

Ahmed! she cried. These things are just stems stuck into the ground. They're not growing plants at all!

He examined the two plants, and gazed at her, feeling sorry for her. The wind was blowing her hair all across her face, and she seemed ready to burst into tears.

They looked so healthy, she said.

Together they went to examine the agapanthus, the tuberoses. The filthy swine! cried Madame. No wonder he didn't want me around while he planted them!

Suddenly she stared at Ahmed. He's coming back. He said he was going to bring me some rose bushes.

He won't dare come back after what he's done, Ahmed declared.

Madame looked even more distraught. And to think – she began, checking herself as she realized that up to a few minutes ago she still had been considering the possibility of dismissing Ahmed and hiring the man. She could not admit to such disloyalty. Ahmed knew what she had stopped herself from saying, and he smiled grimly.

If he comes back, don't let him in. Don't even talk to him. Call me and I'll take care of him.

I'd much prefer that, she said. I don't want to see that disgusting face again.

The wind blew, the dead plants were dumped onto the compost heap, and the brief scandal was no longer mentioned. Ahmed was certain, however, that the man would return.

One day he did. Johara came to the toolshed to say that the bad man was at the door, and Madame was very nervous.

Ahmed put on his djellaba and walked out to the entrance door. He opened it, and looking sternly at the fat man, intoned, as though repeating an order he had learned by rote: Madame said to tell you she knows where you got the flowers, and not to come back here unless you want to explain it to the police.

Then he shut the door and listened while the truck drove

away. Madame was waiting in the doorway of the entrance hall.

He's gone, he said.

Ahmed, what would I do without you? She stared at him for a moment, shaking her head. What did you say to him?

I told him no true Moslem would play tricks on a woman with no husband.

Mrs Pritchard reflected. I'm sure that was exactly the right thing to say. I'm afraid I should have insulted him and gone to bed with a headache afterward. I'm very grateful to you.

Still uneasy because of the deception he had practised upon Madame, and more than a little guilty for having destroyed so many healthy, expensive plants, he found that it made him feel better to say: Everybody plays tricks nowadays, Madame. Everybody.

For him it served as a comforting admission of his wrongdoing, but she took it as a hint. Oh, I shan't do it again, I promise you, she said. He glanced at her approvingly and turned to go.

You're right, Madame, he told her. Don't believe anybody.

The Fqih

One midsummer afternoon a dog went running through a village, stopping just long enough to bite a young man who stood on the main street. It was not a deep wound, and the young man washed it at a fountain nearby and thought no more about it. However, several people who had seen the animal bite him mentioned it to his younger brother. You must take your brother to a doctor in the city, they said.

When the boy went home and suggested this, his brother merely laughed. The next day in the village the boy decided to consult the fqih. He found the old man sitting in the shade under the fig tree in the courtyard of the mosque. He kissed his hand, and told him that a dog no one had ever seen before had bitten his brother and run away.

That's very bad, said the fqih. Have you got a stable you can lock him into? Put him there, but tie his hands behind him. No one must go near him, you understand?

The boy thanked the fqih and set out for home. On the way he determined to cover a hammer with yarn and hit his brother on the back of the head. Knowing that his mother would never consent to seeing her son treated in this way, he decided that it would have to be done when she was away from the house.

That evening while the woman stood outside by the well, he crept up behind his brother and beat him with the hammer until he fell to the floor. Then he fastened his hands behind him and dragged him into a shed next to the house. There he left him lying on the ground, and went out, padlocking the door behind him.

When the brother came to his senses, he began a great outcry. The mother called to the boy: Quick! Run and see what's the matter with Mohammed. But the boy only said: I know what's the matter with him. A dog bit him, and the fqih said he was to stay in the shed.

The woman began to pull at her hair and scratch her face with her fingernails and beat her breasts. The boy tried to calm her, but she pushed him away and ran out to the shed. She put her ear to the door. All she could hear was her son's loud panting as he tried to free his hands from the cords that bound them. She pounded on the wood and screamed his name, but he was struggling, his face in the dirt, and did not reply. Finally the boy led her back to the house. It was written, he told her.

The next morning the woman got astride her donkey and rode to the village to see the fqih. He, however, had left that morning to visit his sister in Rhafsai, and no one knew when he would be back. And so she bought bread and started out on the road for Rhafsai, along with a group of villagers who were on their way to a souq in the region. That night she slept at the souq and the following morning at daybreak she started out again with a different group of people.

Each day the boy threw food in to his brother through a small barred window high above one of the stalls in the shed. The third day he also threw him a knife, so he could cut the ropes and use his hands to eat with. After a while it occurred to him that he had done a foolish thing in giving him the knife, since if he worked long enough with it he might succeed in cutting his way through the door. Thus he threatened to bring no more food until his brother had tossed the knife back through the window.

The mother had no sooner arrived at Rhafsai than she fell ill with a fever. The family with whom she had been travelling took her into their house and cared for her, but it was nearly a month before she was able to rise from the pallet on the floor where she had been lying. By that time the fqih had returned to his village.

Finally she was well enough to start out again. After two

days of sitting on the back of the donkey she arrived home exhausted, and was greeted by the boy.

And your brother? she said, certain that by now he was dead.

The boy pointed to the shed, and she rushed to the door and began to call out to him.

Get the key and let me out! he cried.

I must see the fqih first, aoulidi. Tomorrow.

The next morning she and the boy went to the village. When the fqih saw the woman and her son come into the courtyard he raised his eyes to heaven. It was Allah's will that your son should die as he did, he told her.

But he's not dead! she cried. And he shouldn't stay in there any longer.

The fqih was astounded. Then he said: But let him out! Let him out! Allah has been merciful.

The boy however begged the fqih to come himself and open the door. So they set out, the fqih riding the donkey and the woman and boy following on foot. When they got to the shed, the boy handed the key to the old man, and he opened the door. The young man bounded out, followed by a stench so strong that the fqih shut the door again.

They went to the house, and the woman made tea for them. While they sat drinking, the fqih told the young man: Allah has spared you. You must never mistreat your brother for having shut you away. He did it on my orders.

The young man swore that never would he raise his hand against the boy. But the boy was still afraid, and could not bring himself to look at his brother. When the fqih left to return to the village, the boy went with him, in order to bring back the donkey. As they went along the road, he said to the old man: I'm afraid of Mohammed.

The fqih was displeased. Your brother is older than you, he said. You heard him swear not to touch you.

That night while they were eating, the woman went to the brazier to make the tea. For the first time the boy stole a glance at his brother, and grew cold with fear. Mohammed had swiftly bared his teeth and made a strange sound in his throat. He had done this as a kind of joke, but to the boy it meant something very different.

The fqih should never have let him out, he said to himself. Now he'll bite me, and I'll get sick like him. And the fqih will tell him to throw me into the shed.

He could not bring himself to look again at Mohammed. At night in the dark he lay thinking about it, and he could not sleep. Early in the morning he set out for the village, to catch the fqih before he began to teach the pupils at the msid.

What is it now? asked the fqih.

When the boy told him what he feared, the old man laughed. But he has no disease! He never had any disease, thanks to Allah.

But you yourself told me to lock him up, sidi.

Yes, yes. But Allah has been merciful. Now go home and forget about it. Your brother's not going to bite you.

The boy thanked the fqih and left. He walked through the village and out along the road that led finally to the highway. The next morning he got a ride in a truck that took him all the way to Casablanca. No one in the village ever heard of him again.

The Empty Amulet

Habiba's father, who was the concierge at the principal hotel of the city, provided a comfortable life for his family, but he was unusually strict. Some of Habiba's friends among girls of her age had been to school and even passed their examinations, so that they could become secretaries and bookkeepers and dentists' assistants. Habiba's father, however, considered all this highly immoral, and would not hear of allowing her to attend school. Instead, she learned embroidery and knitting, which she accomplished using modern German machines he bought for her.

When Moumen, a young man of the neighbourhood, came to ask for Habiba's hand in marriage, her father accepted because he knew that the young man worked at a nearby hospital as intern, and thus had permanent employment. Habiba was not consulted. She was delighted to escape from the parental home and the everlasting embroidery.

Since Moumen was a young man with modern ideas, he did not lock his bride into the house when he went out to work. On the contrary, he urged her to get to know the young married women of the quarter. Soon, she was part of a group whose members met each day, first at one house and then another.

Habiba was not long in discovering that the principal topic of conversation amongst these ladies was the state of their health. Every one of them claimed to suffer from some affliction or indisposition. This discountenanced Habiba, for, always having been in the best of health, she could only sit and listen when the subject of ailments arose.

One day she awoke with a headache. When her friends arrived that morning to see her, she complained of the pain. Immediately she was the centre of attention. The following day when they inquired about her health, she told them she still had the pain in her head. And indeed, as she thought about it, it seemed to her that she could feel an occasional throb. Each woman was ready with a different remedy, but they all agreed that a visit to the tomb of Sidi Larbi would provide the surest relief.

There were three other women in the group who were eager to make the pilgrimage. Accordingly, a few days later Habiba went off with them in a large taxi to Sidi Larbi. They took along a picnic lunch, which Habiba, following their advice, washed down with a glass of water containing a large pinch of black earth from outside the mausoleum. Each of them gathered a pile of this dirt to take home for future use. At the end of the day in the open air, Habiba was unable to feel even a trace of headache. Drink the dirt five nights in a row, they told her.

When she got home she hid the packet of earth, knowing that Moumen disapproved of Moroccan medicine. His objections to it were so vehement that she suspected him of being afraid of it, in the same way that she was frightened of entering the hospital where he worked. The nauseating medicinal odours, the bins of bloody bandages, the shining syringes, all filled her with dread.

Scarcely a week passed that some of the young women among her friends did not make a pilgrimage to the tomb of Sidi Hussein or Sidi Larbi or some other not too distant shrine. It seemed to Moumen that Habiba was always on the verge of visiting one saint or another; either she had pains in her back, or cramps, or a stiff neck. Whatever trouble she named, there was always a saint who could cure it.

One evening Moumen went unexpectedly into the kitchen and found Habiba stirring some earth into a glass of water.

Habiba! You can't do that! he cried. It's what they did a hundred years ago.

And two hundred and five hundred, she retorted, her eyes on the glass.

You're a savage! It makes me sick to look at you!

Habiba was unperturbed. She knew he considered the pills and injections used by the Nazarenes superior to the baraka of the saints. This had nothing to do with her, she decided; she was not going to be influenced by him.

I have pains in my side, she said. Rahma had the same pains, and the mud from Sidi Yamani got rid of them in twenty-four hours.

If you'll come to the hospital tomorrow morning, I'll give you some pills, he told her, intending, if she agreed, to hand her some sugar-coated pills containing nothing at all, since he knew her to be in perfect health.

This is my medicine, she said, moving the glass in a circular fashion, to dissolve all the mud.

It cost him an effort not to wrest the glass away from her and dash it to the floor. He shook his head. A beautiful girl like you swallowing dirt!

Habiba leaned back against the sink and calmly drank the contents of the glass.

The day Moumen learned that Habiba was carrying a child, he sat for a long time in a café, trying to think of a way to keep her from going on any more of her absurd pilgrimages. At one point he looked up and noticed a book of cigarette papers that someone had left on the table next to him. He reached over for it. Idly he pulled out two of the little sheets of rice-paper and crumpled them between his fingers. As he glanced down at the tiny ball of paper, the idea came to him.

He paid the qahouaji, and taking the book of cigarette papers with him, he made his way down into the Medina to see a friend who worked as a goldsmith. He wanted him to make a tiny gold cage just big enough to hold a baraka. While they were discussing the size and price of the piece of jewelry, Moumen surreptitiously reached into his pocket and pulled out two cigarette papers, which he rolled into a ball. When they had come to an agreement, he asked the goldsmith for a bit of silk thread, and wound a short length of it around the ball of paper.

Here's the baraka, he told the man, who dropped it into an envelope on which Moumen wrote his name, and promised to have the chain and pendant ready the following afternoon.

The small gold cage on its slender chain made a pretty necklace. When he took it home and fastened it around Habiba's neck, he told her: This baraka is from a very great fqih. It's to protect the baby.

He was a bit ashamed, but greatly relieved, to see how much the gift meant to her. During the months that followed, when she might have been expected to suffer discomfort, she was uncomplaining and happy. She told her friends that her husband did not want her to ride in taxis on country roads because it might be bad for the baby, and they nodded their heads sagely. Besides, said Habiba, I don't need to go any more.

Hamdoul'lah, they said.

The baby was born: a robust little creature who passed through his infancy unscathed by illness. Habiba herself was radiantly healthy; since the day she had begun to wear the cage over her heart she had not once complained of a symptom. It was the possession she valued above all others. The days of making pilgrimages and swallowing mud were far behind; Moumen was pleased with himself for having found such a simple solution to a difficult problem.

One summer afternoon when Habiba rose from her siesta, she took the necklace from the table to fasten it around her neck, for she did not like to be without it. For some reason the chain snapped, and the cage slid to the floor, where it rolled out of sight. As she moved around the room looking for it, she felt a light crunch beneath her foot, and realized that she had stepped on it. The lid had broken off and the ball of paper had tumbled out. She gathered up the broken cage and the baraka that had been inside. The silk thread slipped off and the cigarette papers sprang open.

Habiba uncreased both. Nothing was written on either paper. She held them up to the light and saw the watermarks;

then she understood what they were. She sat perfectly still for a long time, while her sense of injury was slowly replaced by fury with Moumen for having deceived her, and for so long a period of time. When Moumen got home that evening and saw her face, he knew that the hour of reckoning had come. Habiba shouted at him, she wept, she sulked, she said she would never believe him again as long as she lived.

For several days she would not speak to Moumen; when finally one morning she did, it was to announce that she felt dizzy and had pains in her stomach. To his dismay he saw that for the first time she did look ill.

Thanks to your lies I went all that time without any baraka, she said bitterly.

Yes, but you were well all that time, he reminded her.

And that's why I'm sick now! she screamed. It's your fault!

Moumen did not attempt to answer her; he had learned the futility of expecting her to follow a logical train of thought.

Before the week was out, Habiba was on her way to Sidi Larbi with two of her friends. From that time onward Moumen heard nothing from her but an unvarying stream of complaints, cut short only on the day they were divorced.

The Waters of Izli

No one would have guessed, from seeing the two villages spread out there, one higher up than the other on the sunny slope of the mountain, that enmity existed between them. And yet, if you looked closely, you would see certain marked differences in the respective designs they made on the landscape. Tamlat was higher, the houses were farther apart, and there were trees between them. In Izli everything was crowded together, for there was not enough space. The entire village seemed to have been built on top of boulders and at the edges of cliffs. Green fields and meadows surrounded Tamlat. It lay above, where the valley was wide, so that there was ample room for farming, and thus the people lived well. But the orchards down in Izli were little more than steep stairways of terraces. No matter how hard they worked trying to raise vegetables and fruit, the villagers never had enough.

What ought to have helped compensate for Izli's unlucky site was the large spring just outside the village, whose water was the sweetest in the region. The people of Izli claimed great curative powers for it, an idea that was dismissed by the inhabitants of Tamlat, although they themselves often went down and filled their skins and jars with it to take home with them. There was no way of fencing off the land around the spring, or the natives of Izli long ago would have seen to it that no one else had access to the water. If only the people of Tamlat had been willing to admit that the water was superior to their own, eventually they might have been persuaded to trade a few vegetables for it. However, they were careful never to mention it, and except for going casually to fetch it, behaved as if it did not exist.

The man whose land lay nearest to the spring was Ramadi, said to be the most prosperous one in Izli. By the standards of Tamlat he would not have been considered well-off. But his black mare was the only horse in Izli, and his orchard had twenty-three almond trees growing on eight different levels, and on each level he had built a channel that ran with clear water. The mare was a beautiful animal, and he kept her in perfect condition. When he dressed in his white selham and rode the mare through the street out of the village, the people of Izli remarked to each other that he looked almost like Sidi Bouhajja. This was a great compliment, since Sidi Bouhajja was the most important saint in the region. He too wore white garments and rode a black horse, although his was a stallion.

For a long time Ramadi had been on the lookout for a fitting mate for his mare. However, not one stallion among all those he had looked at in the neighbouring villages could be called her equal. In fact, the only horse he would have accepted for her was the shining black stallion ridden by Sidi Bouhajja, and this was out of the question, since there was no way of asking a saint for such a favour.

It was assumed by many people that Sidi Bouhajja and his horse were able to converse together. And it was common knowledge, for he had proclaimed it in public on several occasions, that at the moment of his death it was to be the horse that would decide on his burial place. He asked that his body be fastened astride the animal, which was then to be allowed to go where it pleased. Where it stopped, at that spot Sidi Bouhajja was to be interred. This doubtless lent weight to the belief that the old man and his horse had a secret language between them.

It was a subject for much speculation around the countryside as to which region might prove fortunate enough to witness this event, but everything was cut short by Sidi Bouhajja's sudden collapse one afternoon as he sat outside the mosque at Tamlat.

The saint had ridden up through Izli earlier in the day, passing by Ramadi's house as the mare stood in front of it, shaded by an old olive tree. The stallion wanted to stop, and Sidi Bouhajja had some difficulty in getting him to continue. Ramadi watched, fingering his beard, thinking what a great thing it would be if the stallion should suddenly rise up, saint and all, and mount the mare. Then, feeling ashamed, he looked away.

Later in the day Ramadi got onto the mare and rode up to Tamlat. There in a corner of the market he caught sight of an Aissaoui snake charmer from Izli whom he knew, and he sat down to talk with him. It was then that he heard the news of Sidi Bouhajja's death.

He sat up very straight. The Aissaoui added that soon they would be tying the saint to his horse.

Where do you think it'll go? Ramadi asked him.

It'll probably come here and go into the grain market, the Aissaoui said.

Have you got your snakes with you?

The Aissaoui looked surprised. Yes, I have them, he said.

Get them out there to the turn-off and let him see them, Ramadi told him. He's got to go down the hill instead.

He rose, jumped onto his mare, and rode off.

The Aissaoui ran to the fondouq where he had left his basket of vipers and cobras. Then he hurried up to the corner where the road turned off from the main street and led down the side of the mountain.

Since everyone in Tamlat was watching the elders strap Sidi Bouhajja's body onto the back of the stallion, Ramadi on his mare passed unnoticed as he galloped down the road to Izli. When he got to his house, he left the mare standing under the olive tree and waited.

Up in Tamlat the Aissaoui sat by the edge of the road with his basket. At length he saw the horse come into view, its sacred burden strapped to its back. It cantered down the street toward him, followed at some distance by the elders. He opened his basket and took out two of the larger serpents, holding one in each hand. As the horse approached him, he stood up and made the reptiles writhe in the air. Immediately the horse opened its eyes very wide and turned to the right, down the road leading out of the village.

The Aissaoui put the snakes back into the basket and sauntered out of the bushes which until then had hidden him from the approaching elders. They paid him no attention, and he set out along the road to Izli. Far ahead of him he could see the black form of the stallion racing down the mountainside, the white bundle it carried flopping in the sunlight. After he had walked along for a while, he turned to look back. The elders stood up there at the corner, shading their eyes as they peered down into the valley.

And as Ramadi sat in his doorway waiting, the stallion stormed into the village, stood quiet for an instant, and then trotted directly to Ramadi's house. The mare still stood under the olive tree, switching her tail against the flies. Before anyone arrived to watch, the stallion reared himself up to a great height, bursting the straps that had bound Sidi Bouhajja to his back. The body in the white selham dropped to the ground at the same moment the stallion seized the mare. Ramadi ran forward and pulled it out of the way. Then he returned to the doorway to look on.

A little later some neighbours arrived, and they carried Sidi Bouhajja into Ramadi's courtyard, all the while praising Allah. By the time the men of Tamlat had got down to Izli, the stallion and the mare were standing quietly under the olive tree, and the tolba of Izli chanted inside Ramadi's house.

The men from Tamlat hid their chagrin and accepted the will of Allah. The horse had come to Izli and stopped here, therefore this was where Sidi Bouhajja had to be buried. They helped the men of Izli dig the grave, and the news went out to all the villages around, so that tolba came from many places to chant at the tomb.

It was no time before crowds of pilgrims began to arrive in Izli, seeking baraka at Sidi Bouhajja'a tomb. Soon it was necessary to demolish Ramadi's house and in its place to build a sanctuary where the pilgrims could sleep. At the same time they constructed a domed qoubba over the saint's resting place by the olive tree, and then built a high wall around it. Ramadi was given another house nearby.

Since the pilgrims all carried away with them water from the spring, the water's fame soon spread, and it took on great importance. Even those who did not venerate Sidi Bouhajja came to drink it and take it home with them. In exchange they left offerings of food and money in the sanctuary. Before a year was up, Izli had become more prosperous than Tamlat.

Only Ramadi and the Aissaoui knew of the part they had played in bringing about the stroke of good luck that had changed their village, and they considered it of slight importance, since everything is decided by Allah. What mattered to Ramadi was the beauty of the black colt that now followed the mare wherever he rode her, even if it was down to the plain or up to the market in Tamlat.

Kitty

Kitty lived in a medium-sized house with a big garden around it. She loved some things, like picnics and going to the circus, and she hated other things, like school and going to the dentist's.

One day she asked her mother: "Why is my name Kitty?"

"Your name is really Catherine," her mother said. "We just call you Kitty."

This reply did not satisfy Kitty, and she decided that her mother did not want to tell her the truth. This made her think even more about her name. Finally she thought she had the answer. Her name was Kitty because some day she was going to grow up into a cat. She felt proud of herself for having found this out, and she began to look into the mirror to see if perhaps she was beginning to look like a cat, or at least like a kitten.

For a long time she could see nothing at all but her own pink face. But one day when she went up to the glass she could hardly believe what she saw, for around her mouth tiny grey whiskers were beginning to sprout. She jumped up and down with delight, and waited for her mother to say something about them. Her mother, however, had no time for such things, and so she noticed nothing.

Each day when Kitty looked at her reflection she saw more wonderful changes. Slowly the whiskers grew longer and stood out farther from her face, and a soft grey fur started to cover her skin. Her ears grew pointed and she had soft pads on the palms of her hands and the soles of her feet. All this seemed too good to be true, and Kitty was sad to find that nobody had said a word about the marvellous change in her. One day as she was playing she turned to her mother and said: "Meow. I'm Kitty. Do you like the colour of my fur?"

"I don't know," her mother said. "What colour is it?"

"It's grey!"

"Oh, grey. Very pretty," said her mother, and Kitty saw with a sinking heart that she did not care what colour the fur was.

After that she tried to make several neighbours remark on her fine whiskers, her velvety ears and her short fluffy tail, and they all agreed that these things were very nice, and then paid no more attention to them. Kitty did not care too much. If *they* could not see how different she had become, at least she herself could.

One summer morning when Kitty awoke, she discovered that her fingernails and toenails had been replaced by splendid new pearly grey claws that she could stick out or pull in as she chose. She jumped out of bed and ran into the garden. It was still very early. Her mother and father were asleep, but there were some birds walking around on the lawn.

She slipped behind some bushes and watched. After a long time she began to crawl forward. The branches caught her nightgown, so she tore it off. When one of the birds came very close to her, she sprang forward and caught it. And at that moment she knew that she was no longer a girl at all, and that she would never have to be one again.

The bird tasted good, but she decided not to eat it. Instead, she rolled on her back in the sun and licked her paws. Then she sat up and washed her face. After a while she thought she would go over to Mrs Tinsley's house and see if she could get some breakfast. She climbed up to the top of the wall and ran quickly along it to the roof of the garage. From there she scrambled down the trellis into Mrs Tinsley's backyard. She heard sounds in the kitchen, so she went up to the screen door and looked in. Then she said: "Meow." She had to keep saying it for quite a while before Mrs Tinsley came and saw her.

"Well, if that isn't the cutest kitten!" Mrs Tinsley said, and she called to her husband and her sister. They came and saw the small grey kitten with one paw raised, scratching at the screen. Of course they let her in, and soon Kitty was lapping up a saucer full of milk. She spent the day sleeping, curled up on a cushion, and in the evening she was given a bowl of delicious raw liver.

After dinner she decided to go back home. Mr Tinsley saw her at the kitchen door, but instead of opening the door for her, he picked her up and locked her into the cellar. This was not at all what Kitty wanted, and she cried all night.

In the morning they let her go upstairs, and gave her a big bowl of milk. When she had drunk it she waited in the kitchen until Mrs Tinsley opened the door to go out into the yard. Then she ran as fast as she could between Mrs Tinsley's feet, and climbed up onto the roof of the garage. She looked down at Mrs Tinsley, who was calling: "Kitty, Kitty, Kitty." Then she turned and ran the other way. Soon she was in her own garden. She went up to all the doors and looked in. There were policemen inside the house with her mother and father. They were holding Kitty's torn nightgown in their hands, and her mother was crying and sobbing. No one paid the slightest attention to Kitty.

She went sadly back to Mrs Tinsley's house, and there she stayed for many weeks. Sometimes she would go over to her own house and peek again through the doors, and often she saw her mother or her father. But they looked very different from the way they had looked before, and even if they noticed her, they never came to the door to let her in.

It was nice not having to go to school, and Mr and Mrs Tinsley were very good to her, but Kitty loved her mother and father more than she could love anyone else, and she wanted to be with them.

Mr and Mrs Tinsley let her go out whenever she pleased now, because she always came back. She would go to her house at night and look in through the window to see her father sitting alone reading the paper. This was how she knew that her mother had gone away. Even if she cried and pushed her claws against the window, her father paid no attention to her, and she knew that he would never let her in. Only her mother would do that. She would come and open the door and take her in her arms and rub the fur on her forehead and kiss her.

One day several months later when Kitty climbed over the wall into her own garden, she saw her mother sitting in a chair outside. She looked much better, almost the way she had used to look. Kitty walked slowly toward her mother over the grass, holding her tail in the air. Her mother sat up straighter, watching as she came nearer. Then she put out her hand and wriggled her fingers at Kitty. "Well, the pretty pussycat," she said. "Where did *you* come from?"

Kitty went near enough so that her mother could rub her head and scratch her cheeks. She waved her tail and purred with delight as she felt her mother's fingers stroking her fur. Then she jumped up into her mother's lap and lay curled there, working her claws joyously in and out. After a long time her mother lifted her up and held her against her face, and then she carried her into the house.

That evening Kitty lay happily in her mother's lap. She did not want to try her father's lap because she was afraid he might push her off. Besides, she could see that it would not be very comfortable.

Kitty knew that her mother already loved her, and that her father would learn to love her. At last she was living exactly the life she always had wished for. Sometimes she thought it would be nice if she could make them understand that she was really Kitty, but she knew there was no way of doing that. She never heard them say the word *Kitty* again. Instead, because her fur was so long and fine that when she moved she seemed to be floating, they named her Feather. She had no lessons to worry about, she never had to go to the dentist's, and she no longer had to wonder whether her mother was telling her the truth or not, because she knew the truth. She was Kitty, and she was happy.

Bouayad and the Money

The Aïd el Kebir would be arriving in a month or so.

Each year the sheep cost more, Bouayad told Chaouni. This year they're going to be higher than ever. Why don't we buy twenty and split the cost? When the holiday comes we'll split the proceeds.

Chaouni always had some ready cash. He agreed. They went out to Sidi Yamani and bought the animals cheap from a friend of Bouayad's. They hired a truck to carry them to Tangier. There they put them into a shed at Bouayad's and went together every day, driving them to graze in the country. The sheep had to be fat and beautiful before the Aïd.

One day some soldiers came across the meadow where Bouayad and Chaouni sat watching the sheep. The colonel stopped and looked. Then he went over to Bouayad and asked him if he wanted to sell the sheep.

Maybe, Bouayad said.

The price the colonel offered was exactly what they had been planning to ask in the market. They both thought it would be a good idea to sell them all at once and save themselves the bother of taking them out to pasture every day. The colonel told them to go to his office at the qachla the next morning and he would give them the money. Because he was well-known they did not question his word. The soldiers drove the sheep ahead of them, and Bouayad and Chaouni were left alone in the meadow.

The next day when Bouayad went to the qachla he discovered that the colonel had been called to Rabat. This news made Chaouni decide to go himself the next day. The colonel was still in Rabat. They took turns going to the qachla.

This continued for several weeks. Finally they learned that the colonel was back in Tangier. Now when they went he was not in his office. They were convinced that the colonel had no intention of paying them.

Bouayad was the kind of man who would not admit to having lost. He went to Chaouni and said: Are you with me? Whatever happens? We get that money or we put him out of commission. Are you with me?

No, Chaouni said. I've got a wife and children to think of.

You say good-bye to all that money?

It's gone. I'm sorry I ever listened to you.

That means whatever I get is mine, said Bouayad.

Yes. And the trouble is yours too. You'll be lucky if you stay alive.

It's in the hands of Allah. I'll get the money or you won't see me again.

He went to the Amalat and tried to see the secretary of the governor. The guards refused to let him in. At this point luck began to shine on Bouayad. As he ranted to the guards in front of the office door a man walked past and stopped to listen. Then he spoke to Bouayad. They went outside and Bouayad recounted his tale. The man said: I can help you. Go tomorrow morning to the king's palace at Sidi Amar.

Bouayad did not understand what connection the man could have with the palace, but he trusted him because he had a serious face. The next morning he went up to Sidi Amar and stepped through the open gate. Immediately he was surrounded by soldiers. They asked him again and again why he had walked through the gate. He tried to tell them about the sheep and the appointment he had made the day before outside the Amalat, but they would not stop yanking him this way and that.

Here is where Bouayad's luck became greater than seems possible. The king does not spend even one day a year in Tangier, but he had come from Rabat the day before. Not only was he in residence; he was in the garden not far from the gate, and he saw the commotion. He beckoned to the soldiers to let go of Bouayad so he could approach and present his case.

The king listened until he had finished. Then he told Bouayad to wait, and went down to the palace. As he stood in the garden a man in the uniform of the royal guard walked past Bouayad and smiled at him. He recognized him then as the one who had told him to come to the palace. Later a servant brought out a letter signed by the king, with the instructions that he go to Tetuan and present the letter to the official whose name was on the envelope.

Bouayad did not even stop off at home for lunch. He went straight to the Avenida de España and, sharing a taxi with three others, set out for Tetuan.

Again he was not allowed in. Nor did he trust anyone sufficiently to show him the letter. For several hours he stayed there, insisting that he had a highly secret message that must be delivered to the official by him personally. Finally they allowed him to go inside.

The official took the letter and read it. Then he went into the adjoining room for a moment and returned with the cash for the full amount. Bouayad thanked him.

He went back to Tangier in a state of elation. After his family, the first person he told was Chaouni.

I'm back, he said, and that means I've got the money.

All of it? Chaouni could not believe it.

That's right.

Chaouni said nothing. The next day he went to see Bouayad. I've been thinking. You've got my money too.

Your money? You said good-bye to it. Remember?

Chaouni went home. It was not long before he started a lawsuit against Bouayad, demanding not only his share but Bouayad's as well. When the case was heard, Bouayad was allowed to keep his share. Out of the other half Chaouni was forced to pay a heavy lawyer's fee and Bouayad's fare both to and back from Tetuan.

Rumour and a Ladder

Alone in Paris, Monsieur Ducros sat in his spacious hotel room, preparing to write a letter to his daughter in Kuala Lumpur. He frowned at the hotel stationery, which was now merely printed, instead of being embossed as it had been on his last visit. A symbol of the times, he thought automatically. The slow encroachment of poverty on all sides. Then he glanced down at the cast encasing his leg, smiled briefly at it, and started to write.

My dear Clotilde:

I hope my unwonted silence hasn't disturbed you. Ordinarily I'm a good correspondent; admit it. I can't believe Kuala Lumpur has altered much since 1965. As you know, it was my last post. I was pleased to hear that Abd er Rahman and his wife are still there; one never knows. I passed my eighty-fifth birthday quietly in Tangier. In a moment you will see what I mean by "quietly".

The incredible irony of certain situations in which life insists upon involving us! What was I doing, standing at the top of a stepladder in the library on a Sunday morning? You may well ask. I also asked myself that, but a good deal too late.

When I felt the ladder tilting (for this is the way it all began) and knew I was going to fall, I was aware of several things simultaneously: that everything was unfinished; that I had been an idiot to climb up there; that people would believe I had been drunk or the victim of an assault (suppositions equally damaging to one's posthumous repu-

144

tation in that vicious city where, as you're aware, no one thinks well of anyone); and above all the conviction that everything would go wrong, with the result that you and Pierrot somehow would not be able to inherit El Hafa. Because, my girl, I was certain that it was the end. Then the leg got involved with the ladder as we went down, there was a crash, and I lay there, my head pounding, and quite aware that my leg was broken above the knee. Fortunately the big Chichaoua rug was underneath, or I should have hit marble. I called endlessly for Annamaria. When she finally appeared, she claimed the wind was rattling the shutters so hard that she hadn't heard me at first. It's true that her room faces northeast, and there was a gale blowing outside. Still –

I had her send Abdeslam on foot to Dr Rinaldi's clinic. (The telephone had been out of order for more than three weeks.) Rinaldi arrived. The femur was fractured. He saw the stepladder by the bookshelves, and looked at me reprovingly. Off I went to the clinic; in traction for what seemed an eternity. Actually it was something less than a month and a half. . . .

II

It's essential that I go to Paris, said Monsieur Ducros, surveying his leg, still in its cast. As you can see, I manage perfectly well now with the cane.

Dr Rinaldi shrugged. Luck has been with you so far, he said. Why shouldn't we expect it to continue?

They sat sipping whisky in the library where the accident had taken place. After a certain hesitation Dr Rinaldi inquired if the rumour were true that his host planned to sell El Hafa.

Monsieur Ducros bristled. But what an idea! Certainly not! I haven't the slightest intention of selling. I know that Saudi is interested, and the offer would be generous. I intend my daughter and her husband to have the property after my death. I've spent all my retired years in this house, and everything I own in the world is in it.

Dr Rinaldi looked around the room approvingly. There are many treasures, yes. Astonishing how Japanese, Tibetan, Khmer and Persian can blend in a room.

Not really, if you think about it, said Monsieur Ducros, without elaborating. The point is, I don't want to give up anything. You understand. With my things around me, it's as though I were still out there in the Far East. I enjoy my little life, and I can assure you I have no intention of interrupting it by selling El Hafa.

There's one thing I'm curious about, Dr Rinaldi said after a moment. Those paintings at the far end of the hall. I couldn't help noticing them.

Monsieur Ducros chuckled. Yes, it's a jarring note, I know. But they're not really much in evidence. I keep it fairly dark at that end, purposely. Madame Ducros bought those things shortly after the First World War. They say less than nothing to me, I confess. I've been told they have a certain value, but I don't take that too seriously. I've kept them because my wife was so fond of them.

A Moroccan in a white dinner jacket announced that dinner was served. Dr Rinaldi handed Monsieur Ducros his cane, and they rose from their chairs.

At the table Monsieur Ducros pointed to the carafes in the centre, saying: The white is simply Valpierre. The red is a fairly good Bordeaux. You've taken Mademoiselle Herzler's tray up, Abdeslam?

When they were alone in the dining-room, he spoke confidentially: My secretary insists upon eating by herself in her room. I think she's not entirely happy here. She objects very much to the wind. Swiss, he added, as if by way of explanation.

Dr Rinaldi, busying himself with his sole meunière, did not reply. Presently he looked up and said with great seriousness: I suspect you of grossly underestimating the worth of those canvases. May I ask what you imagine they'd fetch on the market today?

Monsieur Ducros stopped eating, and thought for a moment. I have no idea, he said.

For the five Soutines alone I can get you two million French francs tomorrow. As he made the statement he stared fixedly at his host, as if to measure his reaction. He saw a flash of interest, followed immediately by disbelief.

Ridiculous. They're not Titians, after all.

I'm entirely serious.

Monsieur Ducros was quiet. Then he sighed. Even if your estimate is not dramatically exaggerated, and even if I wanted to dispose of them, what would be the point? The money would be of no use here, and it couldn't be taken out of Morocco.

Oh, come, said Dr Rinaldi. There are ways.

No, thank you, Monsieur Ducros said firmly. The law is generally illogical and often unjust, but I'm not one to flout it.

My friend, you function according to the ethos of a bygone era. But I approve, I approve.

In my experience the rational man is the one who obeys the law.

But alas! sighed Dr Rinaldi. How human it is to be irrational!

Monsieur Ducros glanced furtively at his guest: he suspected these last words to be a veiled reference to his accident. The doctor already had upbraided him severely for allowing the absurd thing to happen. What were servants for, if not to climb stepladders? He had not mentioned Monsieur Ducros's age, but this show of discretion counted for little because of the stern manner in which he had voiced his opinion. Monsieur Ducros recognized the minatory tone; since he had passed his eightieth birthday all his doctors had used it with him.

They spoke of other things. But later, over coffee and Armagnac in the den, Monsieur Ducros turned with a puzzled expression to his guest.

To return for a moment to the subject of those paintings. How would your buyer have arranged to get them out of the country? I'm curious.

The question wouldn't have arisen, the doctor told him. An American collector is building a house in Marrakesh. Why? Are you tempted?

Monsieur Ducros shook his head. No, no! Not in the least.

III

Their next encounter, less than a week later, was unexpected and tempestuous. In the middle of a weekday afternoon, Monsieur Ducros was brought by a taxi-driver to Dr Rinaldi's clinic in a state bordering on apoplexy. The cast on his leg had been split open, and tatters of gauze trailed out from inside it.

Seeing that Monsieur Ducros was not in a state to speak coherently, Dr Rinaldi questioned the taxi-driver. He was struck by a car?

The driver did not know. He had been summoned by an official at the airport and instructed to take the passenger home, but on the way the old man had demanded to be brought to the clinic.

Monsieur Ducros was put to bed and given an injection. Later that evening, after an enforced sleep of several hours, he was sufficiently rested to tell his tale to Dr Rinaldi.

Abdeslam had driven him to the airport, given his luggage to a porter, and left. The plane for Paris arrived. As his passport was being examined, a man had appeared from nowhere, and asked him to go with him into an inner office, where he and two others had made him undress. Not content with that, they had refused to believe that his leg was broken, and had held him by force while they smashed open the cast and pulled the inside to pieces in search for money.

It's that rumour! They had the effrontery to tell me they were acting on secret information that I'd sold El Hafa.

Dr Rinaldi was deeply shocked. Unheard-of! Herbier must be informed immediately at the consulate.

I shall sue for damages! Monsieur Ducros cried feebly.

My poor friend, that would produce an enormous zero. You've lived here long enough to realize that. All you can do is accept what has happened, be sure the leg is all right, put on a new cast, and start out again.

Monsieur Ducros shut his eyes for a moment, and opened them again. You can help me, he said.

Naturally. As your doctor I can attest to the authenticity of the fracture. Perhaps they'd like to see the X-ray, too, he added acidly.

Monsieur Ducros did not seem to be listening. He was looking at the ceiling. Yes, you can help me, he repeated.

Dr Rinaldi decided that the time had come for his patient to rest. You can count on me, he told him.

The next day he went into the sickroom and announced that he was ready to make a new cast. Monsieur Ducros waved him away. No, no. I don't want it.

But you must have a cast. You can't walk without one.

I shan't walk. I'll stay in my bed at home until you come to do it.

As you like, Dr Rinaldi said shortly, feeling that he was being foolish to humour the caprice of an unreasonable old man.

Abdeslam can take me home this afternoon. Will you come by at five o'clock?

Fleetingly the idea occurred to the doctor that the experience at the airport might have caused a small cerebral lesion. In some subtle way Monsieur Ducros's personality seemed very slightly altered.

You must not use the leg, he said frowning. Not even to take a few steps in your room. Are we agreed?

IV

At El Hafa Dr Rinaldi found his patient propped up in an enormous antique bed; the damask curtains that hung from the baldaquin overhead nearly hid him from view.

I've obeyed you to the letter, he called out, even before the doctor and his assistant had got inside the room.

Dr Rinaldi laughed. When do you plan your next escape attempt?

I haven't thought about it, said Monsieur Ducros. May I have a five-minute conversation with you in private?

Dr Rinaldi spoke with the Moroccan, and he left the room. When they were alone, Monsieur Ducros leaned forward and beckoned to the other to approach.

I'll explain, he whispered. You see, I don't want you to put the cast on today. I merely wanted you to come by. And I've decided to sell those paintings, if you can get in touch with the American.

This inconsequential coupling of ideas confirmed Dr Rinaldi's previous suspicions; he saw in it a clear instance of mental dysfunction. Come, he said, sitting down on the edge of the bed. One thing at a time. May I ask why you prefer to remain without the cast?

Because I must know whether or not the paintings can be sold. I should think that would be obvious.

I hadn't connected the two things, the doctor said drily. But since what interests you most is evidently the sale of the paintings, I can say: yes, they definitely can be sold, and in short order, if you like. I myself will buy them and resell them.

At a reasonable profit, I hope, added Monsieur Ducros, smiling.

Very likely.

You said two million, as I recall.

Dr Rinaldi laughed. If you want to throw in the Vlaminck, the Rouault and the Kokoschka, two and a quarter.

Monsieur Ducros threw up his hands. Kokoschka, indeed! I don't know one from the other. They're all equally inept. That would make all eight of them, wouldn't it? I have some old Thai things I'll hang at that end of the hall. They'll be far more in keeping.

Dr Rinaldi looked searchingly at his patient. This is serious? You really want my cheque now?

But not at all! The currency. In French francs.

Dr Rinaldi opened his mouth. But, he began.

You don't agree?

It will take time. Perhaps by tomorrow evening.

Monsieur Ducros was waving his hands again. Just bring the francs here to me.

Shaking his head with disapproval, Dr Rinaldi said: Far too much money to leave lying around the house.

This seemed to mystify Monsieur Ducros. Surely you've understood by now what I expect you to do with the banknotes? You'll build them into the cast. And what they imagined was happening the first time will actually happen this time.

After a long silence Dr Rinaldi said slowly: You can scarcely expect me to be eager to risk my professional status simply to help you perpetrate a fraud.

Monsieur Ducros cried excitedly: Fraud! I've already been punished. Now I want to *deserve* that punishment!

The doctor stood up. I find it quite extraordinary, the total change in your views on morality.

Nothing has changed. What was a question of ethics has become a question of honour.

As Dr Rinaldi moved around the room, following the patterns of the rug, he said: You realize how much more work it would mean for me, having to do it all without my assistant?

Monsieur Ducros, knowing he had won, pressed on. Herbier has been in touch with Rabat, no? He has a formal apology for the incident. There's absolutely no question of a repetition. The element of risk has been removed.

The doctor returned to the bed and placed his hands on the footboard. I retract what I said about you at dinner not too long ago. You are indeed a product of our times.

I don't see it that way at all, Monsieur Ducros said quickly. This little ploy of revenge in no way affects my point of view. We're playing a game of extra-legal tit-for-tat, nothing more.

It's quite all right, said Dr Rinaldi. You won't need any medical attestations if Herbier himself is accompanying you to the airport.

. . . And that is the bare outline of how your father took the first step along the pathway to crime. But criminals can be fiercely fond of their families, you know. So, go to the Hong Kong and Shanghai Bank in Kuala and ask for Mister Nigel Dawson. He will explain to you that you now have an account with them, and that it has seventy-five thousand British pounds in it at the moment. I'm sure there are many things for which it will be useful, including, I hope, a visit by you and Pierrot to Tangier before too long.

I had the paintings thanks to your mother. And I think she would appreciate the ridiculous turn of events which made it possible for me to sell them for a small fortune. But luck is always absurd.

I imagine you sitting in the dubious freshness of that air-conditioned apartment, looking down at the wet trees and traffic of "*Kuala l'impur*", as Cocteau called it. But there are places far more impure!

Know that I think of you, and, I beg you, let me have news soon.

ton père qui t'aime

The Eye

Ten or twelve years ago there came to live in Tangier a man who would have done better to stay away. What happened to him was in no way his fault, notwithstanding the whispered innuendos of the English-speaking residents. These people often have reactions similar to those of certain primitive groups: when misfortune overtakes one of their number, the others by mutual consent refrain from offering him aid, and merely sit back to watch, certain that he has called his suffering down upon himself. He has become taboo, and is incapable of receiving help. In the case of this particular man, I suppose no one could have been of much comfort; still, the tacit disapproval called forth by his bad luck must have made the last months of his life harder to bear.

His name was Duncan Marsh, and he was said to have come from Vancouver. I never saw him, nor do I know anyone who claims to have seen him. By the time his story reached the cocktail-party circuit he was dead, and the more irresponsible residents felt at liberty to indulge their taste for myth-making.

He came alone to Tangier, rented a furnished house on the slopes of Djamaa el Mokra – they were easy enough to find in those days, and correspondingly inexpensive – and presently installed a teen-age Moroccan on the premises to act as a night-watchman. The house provided a resident cook and gardener, but both of these were discharged from their duties, the cook being replaced by a woman brought in at the suggestion of the watchman. It was not long after this that Marsh felt the first symptoms of a digestive illness which over the months grew steadily worse. The doctors in Tangier advised him to go to London. Two months in hospital there helped him somewhat. No clear diagnosis was made, however, and he returned here only to become bedridden. Eventually he was flown back to Canada on a stretcher, and succumbed there shortly after his arrival.

In all this there was nothing extraordinary; it was assumed that Marsh had been one more victim of slow poisoning by native employees. There have been several such cases during my five decades in Tangier. On each occasion it has been said that the European victim had only himself (or herself) to blame, having encouraged familiarity on the part of a servant. What strikes the outsider as strange is that no one ever takes the matter in hand and inaugurates a search for the culprit, but in the total absence of proof there is no point in attempting an investigation.

Two details complete the story. At some point during his illness Marsh told an acquaintance of the arrangements he had made to provide financial aid for his night-watchman in the event that he himself should be obliged to leave Morocco; he had given him a notarized letter to that effect, but apparently the boy never tried to press his claim. The other report came from Dr Halsey, the physician who arranged for Marsh's removal from the house to the airport. It was this last bit of information which, for me, at least, made the story take on life. According to the doctor, the soles of Marsh's feet had been systematically marked with deep incisions in the form of crude patterns; the cuts were recent, but there was some infection. Dr Halsey called in the cook and the watchman: they showed astonishment and dismay at the sight of their employer's feet, but were unable to account for the mutilations. Within a few days after Marsh's departure, the original cook and gardener returned to take up residence, the other two having already left the house.

The slow poisoning was classical enough, particularly in the light of Marsh's remark about his provision for the boy's well-being, but the knife-drawn designs on the feet somehow got in the way of whatever combinations of motive one could invent. I thought about it. There could be little doubt that the boy was guilty. He had persuaded Marsh to get rid of the cook that came with the house, even though her wages had to continue to be paid, and to hire another woman (very likely from his own family) to do the cooking. The poisoning process lasts many months if it is to be undetectable, and no one is in a better position to take charge of it than the cook herself. Clearly she knew about the financial arrangement that had been made for the boy, and expected to share in it. At the same time the crosses and circles slashed in the feet were inexplicable. The slow poisoner is patient, careful, methodical; his principal concerns are to keep the dosage effective and to avoid leaving any visible marks. Bravado is unknown to him.

The time came when people no longer told the story of Duncan Marsh. I myself thought of it less often, having no more feasible hypotheses to supply. One evening perhaps five years ago, an American resident here came to me with the news that he had discovered a Moroccan who claimed to have been Marsh's night-watchman. The man's name was Larbi; he was a waiter at Le Fin Bec, a small back-street restaurant. Apparently he spoke poor English, but understood it without difficulty. This information was handed me for what it was worth, said the American, in the event that I felt inclined to make use of it.

I turned it over in my mind, and one night a few weeks later I went down to the restaurant to see Larbi for myself. The place was dimly lit and full of Europeans. I studied the three waiters. They were interchangeable, with wide black moustaches, blue jeans and sports shirts. A menu was handed to me; I could scarcely read it, even directly under the glow of the little table lamp. When the man who had brought it returned, I asked for Larbi.

He pulled the menu from my hand and left the table. A moment later another of the triumvirate came up beside me and handed me the menu he carried under his arm. I ordered in Spanish. When he brought the soup I murmured that I was surprised to find him working there. This brought him up short; I could see him trying to remember me.

"Why wouldn't I be working here?" His voice was level, without inflection.

"Of course! Why not? It was just that I thought by now you'd have a bazaar or some sort of shop."

His laugh was a snort. "Bazaar!"

When he arrived with the next course, I begged his pardon for meddling in his affairs. But I was interested, I said, because for several years I had been under the impression that he had received a legacy from an English gentleman.

"You mean Señor Marsh?" His eyes were at last wide open.

"Yes, that was his name. Didn't he give you a letter? He told his friends he had."

He looked over my head as he said: "He gave me a letter."

"Have you ever showed it to anyone?" This was tactless, but sometimes it is better to drive straight at the target.

"Why? What good is it? Señor Marsh is dead." He shook his head with an air of finality, and moved off to another table. By the time I had finished my crème caramel, most of the diners had left, and the place seemed even darker. He came over to the table to see if I wanted coffee. I asked for the check. When he brought it I told him I should like very much to see the letter if he still had it.

"You can come tomorrow night or any night, and I'll show it to you. I have it at home."

I thanked him and promised to return in two or three days. I was confused as I left the restaurant. It seemed clear that the waiter did not consider himself to be incriminated in Duncan Marsh's troubles. When, a few nights later, I saw the document, I no longer understood anything.

It was not a letter; it was a *papier timbré* of the kind on sale at tobacconists. It read, simply: *To Whom It May Concern: I, Duncan Whitelow Marsh, do hereby agree to deposit the sum of One Hundred Pounds to the account of Larbi Lairini, on the first of each month, for as long as I live.* It was signed and notarized in the presence of two Moroccan witnesses, and bore the date June

11, 1966. As I handed it back to him I said: "And it never did you any good."

He shrugged and slipped the paper into his wallet. "How was it going to? The man died."

"It's too bad."

"*Suerte*." In the Moroccan usage of the word, it means *fate*, rather than simple luck.

At that moment I could have pressed on, and asked him if he had any idea as to the cause of Marsh's illness, but I wanted time for considering what I had just learned. As I rose to leave I said: "I'm sorry it turned out that way. I'll be back in a few days." He held out his hand and I shook it. I had no intentions then. I might return soon or I might never go back.

For as long as I live. The phrase echoed in my mind for several weeks. Possibly Marsh had worded it that way so it would be readily understandable to the *adoul* of Tangier who had affixed their florid signatures to the sheet; yet I could not help interpreting the words in a more melodramatic fashion. To me the document represented the officializing of a covenant already in existence between master and servant: Marsh wanted the watchman's help, and the watchman had agreed to give it. There was nothing upon which to base such an assumption, nevertheless I thought I was on the right track. Slowly I came to believe that if only I could talk to the watchman, in Arabic, and inside the house itself, I might be in a position to see things more clearly.

One evening I walked to Le Fin Bec and without taking a seat motioned to Larbi to step outside for a moment. There I asked him if he could find out whether the house Señor Marsh had lived in was occupied at the moment or not.

"There's nobody living there now." He paused and added: "It's empty. I know the guardian."

I had decided, in spite of my deficient Arabic, to speak to him in his own language, so I said: "Look. I'd like to go with you to the house and see where everything happened. I'll give you fifteen thousand francs for your trouble."

He was startled to hear the Arabic; then his expression

shifted to one of satisfaction. "He's not supposed to let anyone in," he said.

I handed him three thousand francs. "You arrange that with him. And fifteen for you when we leave the house. Could we do it Thursday?"

The house had been built, I should say, in the fifties, when good construction was still possible. It was solidly embedded in the hillside, with the forest towering behind it. We had to climb three flights of stairs through the garden to get to the entrance. The guardian, a squinting Djibli in a brown djellaba, followed close on our footsteps, eyeing me with mistrust.

There was a wide terrace above, with a view to the southeast over the town and the mountains. Behind the terrace a shadowed lawn ended where the forest began. The living room was large and bright, with French doors giving onto the lawn. Odours of damp walls and mildew weighted the air. The absurd conviction that I was about to understand everything had taken posession of me; I noticed that I was breathing more quickly. We wandered into the dining-room. There was a corridor beyond, and the room where Marsh had slept, shuttered and dark. A wide curving stairway led down to a level where there were two more bedrooms, and continued its spiral to the kitchen and servants' rooms below. The kitchen door opened onto a small flagstoned patio where high phylodendron covered the walls.

Larbi looked out and shook his head. "That's the place where all the trouble began," he said glumly.

I pushed through the doorway and sat down on a wrought-iron bench in the sun. "It's damp inside. Why don't we stay out here?"

The guardian left us and locked up the house. Larbi squatted comfortably on his heels near the bench.

There would have been no trouble at all, he said, if only Marsh had been satisfied with Yasmina, the cook whose wages were included in the rent. But she was a careless worker and the food was bad. He asked Larbi to find him another cook.

"I told him ahead of time that this woman Meriam had a little girl, and some days she could leave her with friends and some days she would have to bring her with her when she came to work. He said it didn't matter, but he wanted her to be quiet."

The woman was hired. Two or three days a week she came accompanied by the child, who would play in the patio where she could watch her. From the beginning Marsh complained that she was noisy. Repeatedly he sent messages down to Meriam, asking her to make the child be still. And one day he went quietly around the outside of the house and down to the patio. He got on all fours, put his face close to the little girl's face, and frowned at her so fiercely that she began to scream. When Meriam rushed out of the kitchen he stood up smiling and walked off. The little girl continued to scream and wail in a corner of the kitchen, until Meriam took her home. That night, still sobbing, she came down with a high fever. For several weeks she hovered between life and death, and when she was finally out of danger she could no longer walk.

Meriam, who was earning relatively high wages, consulted one fqih after another. They agreed that "the eye" had been put on the child; it was equally clear that the Nazarene for whom she worked had done it. What they told her she must do, Larbi explained, was to administer certain substances to Marsh which eventually would make it possible to counteract the spell. This was absolutely necessary, he said, staring at me gravely. Even if the señor had agreed to remove it (and of course she never would have mentioned it to him) he would not have been able to. What she gave him could not harm him; it was merely medicine to relax him so that when the time came to undo the spell he would not make any objections.

At some point Marsh confided to Larbi that he suspected Meriam of slipping soporifics into his food, and begged him to be vigilant. The provision for Larbi's well-being was signed as an inducement to enlisting his active support. Since to Larbi the mixtures Meriam was feeding her master were relatively harmless, he reassured him and let her continue to dose him with her concoctions.

Tired of squatting, Larbi suddenly stood up and began to

walk back and forth, stepping carefully in the centre of each flagstone. "When he had to go to the hospital in London, I told her: 'Now you've made him sick. Suppose he doesn't come back? You'll never break it.' She was worried about it. 'I've done what I could,' she said. 'It's in the hands of Allah.'"

When Marsh did return to Tangier, Larbi urged her to be quick about bringing things to a head, now that she had been fortunate enough to get him back. He was thinking, he said, that it might be better for the señor's health if her treatment were not continued for too long a time.

I asked no questions while he talked; I made a point of keeping my face entirely expressionless, thinking that if he noticed the least flicker of disapproval he might stop. The sun had gone behind the trees and the patio was chilly. I had a strong desire to get up and walk back and forth as he was doing, but I thought even that might interrupt him. Once stopped, the flow might not resume.

Soon Marsh was worse than ever, with racking pains in his abdomen and kidneys. He remained in bed then, and Larbi brought him his food. When Meriam saw that he was no longer able to leave his bed, even to go into the bathroom, she decided that the time had come to get rid of the spell. On the same night that a fqih held a ceremony at her house in the presence of the crippled child, four men from Meriam's family came up to Djamaa el Mokra.

"When I saw them coming, I got onto my motorcycle and went into the city. I didn't want to be here when they did it. It had nothing to do with me."

He stood still and rubbed his hands together. I heard the southwest wind beginning to sound in the trees; it was that time of afternoon. "Come. I'll show you something," he said.

We climbed steps around the back of the house and came out onto a terrace with a pergola over it. Beyond this lay the lawn and the wall of trees.

"He was very sick for the next two days. He kept asking me to telephone the English doctor."

"Didn't you do it?"

Larbi stopped walking and looked at me. "I had to clean everything up first. Meriam wouldn't touch him. It was during the rains. He had mud and blood all over him when I got back here and found him. The next day I gave him a bath and changed the sheets and blankets. And I cleaned the house, because they got mud everywhere when they brought him back in. Come on. You'll see where they had to take him."

We had crossed the lawn and were walking in the long grass that skirted the edge of the woods. A path led off to the right through the tangle of undergrowth, and we followed it, climbing across boulders and fallen treetrunks until we came to an old stone well. I leaned over the wall of rocks around it and saw the small circle of sky far below.

"They had to drag him all the way here, you see, and hold him steady right over the well while they made the signs on his feet, so the blood would fall into the water. It's no good if it falls on the side of the well. And they had to make the same signs the fqih drew on paper for the little girl. That's hard to do in the dark and in the rain. But they did it. I saw the cuts when I bathed him."

Cautiously I asked him if he saw any connection between all this and Marsh's death. He ceased staring into the well and turned around. We started to walk back toward the house.

"He died because his hour had come."

And had the spell been broken? I asked him. Could the child walk afterward? But he had never heard, for Meriam had gone to Kenitra not much later to live with her sister.

When we were in the car, driving back down to the city, I handed him the money. He stared at it for several seconds before slipping it into his pocket.

I let him off in town with a vague sense of disappointment, and I saw that I had not only expected, but actually hoped, to find someone on whom the guilt might be fixed. What constitutes a crime? There was no criminal intent – only a mother moving in the darkness of ancient ignorance. I thought about it on my way home in the taxi.

At the Krungthep Plaza

It was the day when the President of the United States was due to arrive with his wife on a visit to the King and Queen. Throughout the preceding afternoon squads of men had been running up and down the boulevard, dragging with them heavy iron stands to be used as barricades along the kerbs. Mang Huat rose from his bed sweaty and itching, having slept very little during the night. Ever since he had been advised that the procession would be passing in front of the hotel he had been awaiting the day with mounting dread. The smallest incident could jeopardize his career. It needed only one lunatic with a hand grenade.

With distaste he pulled aside the curtains near his bed and peered out into the light of the inauspicious day. Later, when he had showered, he returned to the window and stood for a long time. Above the city the grey sky was ahum with helicopters; so far none had hit the tops of the highest chedis towering above the temples, but people in the street watched with interest each time an object clattered overhead in the direction of a nearby spire. At times, when a police car was on its way through the quarter, all traffic was suspended, and there would follow an unusual, disturbing hush in which he could only hear the whirr of the insects in the trees. Then there would come other sounds of life, farther away: the cries of children and the barking of dogs, and they too were disturbing, these naked noises in place of the unceasing roar of motors.

No one seemed to know when the royal cortège would go

by. The radio had announced the time as ten o'clock, but gossip in the lobby downstairs, reportedly straight from police headquarters, fixed the starting hour as noon. Mang Huat decided not to have breakfast, nor indeed to eat at all until the danger had passed and he was free from tension.

He sat behind his desk tapping the point of an eyetooth with his fingernail, and looking thoughtfully across at Miss Pakun as she typed. The magenta silk curtains at his office windows stirred slightly with the breath of an oscillating fan. They gave the room a boudoir glow in which a motion or a posture sometimes could seem strangely ambivalent. Today the phenomenon, rather than stimulating him, merely increased the distrust he had been feeling with regard to his secretary. She was unusually attractive and efficient, but he had to tell himself that this was not the point. He had engaged her in what he considered good faith, assuming that the information she had written on her application form was true. He had chosen her from among several other equally presentable applicants because she bore the stamp of a good bourgeois upbringing.

His equivocal feelings about Miss Pakun dated from the previous week, when his cashier, Udom by name, had reported seeing her walking along the street in an unsanitary and disreputable quarter of Thonburi on the other side of the river. Udom knew the area well; it was a neighbourhood of shacks, mounds of garbage, opium houses and brothels. If she lived over there, why had she given the Sukhumvit address? And if not, what legitimate excuse could she have for visiting this unsavoury part of the city? He had even wondered if Pakun was her true name.

Mang Huat was proud of his three-room suite at the Krungthep Plaza. At thirty-two he was the manager of the hotel, and that pleased him. Through a small window in the wall of his salon he could, if he felt so inclined, look down into the lobby and see what was happening in almost every corner of it. He never used the peephole. It was enough that the staff knew of its existence.

From where he sat he could hear the trickle of the fountain in the next room. A friend, recently moved to Hong Kong, had left it with him, and he had spent a good deal of money getting it installed. Miss Pakun coughed, probably to remind him that he was smoking. She always coughed when he smoked. On a few occasions when she had first come to work for him he had put out his cigarette. Today he was not much concerned with the state of her throat. Nor, he thought, did he care whether she lived at the elegant address in Sukhumvit or in a slum alley of Thonburi. He no longer had any intention of forging an intimate friendship with her.

Later in the morning Udom knocked on his door. Udom was a friend from university days, down on his luck, who had begged for work at the hotel. Mang Huat, persuaded that it was unrealistic to expect any man to possess more than one good quality, had given the job of cashier to Udom, who was unreliable but honest.

Ever since his uncle's partner had placed him in his present exalted position, Mang Huat had experienced the bliss of feeling sheltered from the outside world. Today for the first time that delicious peace of mind was being threatened. It was absurd, he knew; there was little likelihood of an accident, but any situation beyond his control caused him undue anxiety.

Udom came over to the desk and murmured gloomily that the American Security men were downstairs asking for a passkey to the rooms. I told them I'd have to speak to you, he went on. It's not obligatory, you know. Only the keys of certain specific rooms, if they ask for them.

I know that, said Mang Huat. Give them a passkey.

The guests are going to object.

Mang Huat bridled. What difference does that make? Give them whatever keys they ask for. Just be sure you get them all back.

It scandalized him that anyone should hesitate to accept this added protection, but then Udom could be counted on to create complications and find objections. Mang Huat suspected that he had not entirely outgrown his youthful Marxist sympathies, and sometimes he wondered if it had been wise to take him on to the staff.

Pangs of hunger were making his nervousness more acute. It was twenty-five minutes past one. Miss Pakun had not yet returned from lunch. All at once he realized that a new sound which filled the air outside had been going on for some time. He stepped to the window. The big official cars were rolling past, and at a surprising speed. His eye suddenly caught the two white Bentleys from the palace, enclosed by their escort of motorcycles. He held his breath until they were gone. Even then he listened for a minute before he telephoned to order his lunch.

Late in the afternoon the receptionist rang his office to say that a guest was demanding to see him. Suddenly the threat was there again. I can't see anyone, he said, and hung up.

Five minutes later Udom was on the wire. I was afraid this would happen, he said. An Englishman is complaining that the police searched his room.

Tell him I'm not in my office, said Mang Huat. And to Miss Pakun: No incoming calls. You hear?

Twilight had come down all at once, brought on by a great black cloud that swelled above the city. The thought occurred to him that he could let Miss Pakun go now, before the rain came. He stood at the window staring out. The city sparkled with millions of extra lights; they were looped in fanciful designs through the branches of the trees across the canal. A triumphal arch had been built over the entrance to the bridge, spectacularly floodlighted in red and blue to show a thirty-foot-high face of the visiting president, with appropriate words of welcome beneath, in English and Thai.

The buzzer in the antechamber sounded. Miss Pakun answered it, and a bellboy in scarlet uniform came in with a note on a tray. He's had smallpox, Mang Huat said to himself. Who can have hired him? On his pad he scribbled a reminder to have the boy discharged in the morning, and took the note from him. Udom had written: *The man is in the bar getting the guests to sign a petition. I think you should see him.*

Mang Huat read the note twice in disbelief. Then he pounded the desk once with his fist, and Miss Pakun glanced up. Because he was angry, he reminded himself that above all he must keep his composure. With such malcontents it was imperative to be adamant, and not to allow oneself to be drawn into discussion, much less argument.

The buzzer sounded. Tell him I'll be free in five minutes, he said to Miss Pakun.

There was no longer any question of letting her go before the storm broke. She would simply have to take her shoes off, like other people in that squalid quarter where she surely lived, and wade barefoot through the puddles and ponds, to the end of the alley where a taxi could not take her. In a moment she came back in and sat down, patting her hair and smoothing her skirt. At that moment a police car must have been in the neighbourhood, for there was one of the sudden ominous silences outside. While Miss Pakun carefully applied a whole series of cosmetics to her features, he sat in the stillness and heard a gecko chatter beyond the air-conditioning box behind him; the tentative chirruping pierced the slight whirr of the motor. And the insects in the trees still droned. He was sorry he had made a time limit. The five minutes of silence seemed like twenty. When the time was up Miss Pakun, resplendent, rose once more and turned to go out. Mang Huat stopped her.

No typing, please, while the man is here, he said crisply. Only shorthand. You can do it. (Her face had begun to change its expression.) This is an agitator, he stressed. We must have a record of everything he says.

Miss Pakun always grew timid and claimed insufficient knowledge of English if he asked her to transcribe a conversation in that language. The results of her work, however, were generally successful. Mang Huat glowered. You must get every word. He may threaten me.

The visitor came in, followed by Miss Pakun. He was young, and looked like a university student. With a brief smile he sat down in a chair facing Mang Huat, and said: Thank you for letting me in.

Mang Huat took this as sarcasm. You came to complain?

You see, the young man began, I'm trying to get an extension of my tourist visa without leaving the country.

Mang Huat slapped the desk hard with the flat of his hand. Someone has made a mistake. You are looking for the Immigration Department. My secretary will give you the address.

The young man raised his voice. I was trying to lead up to my complaint. But I'll make it now. It's an affront to your guests to allow the Americans into the rooms.

Ah! Perhaps you should complain to the Thai police, Mang Huat suggested, standing up to show that the meeting was at an end. My secretary can also give you that address.

The young Englishman stared at him for an instant with patent disgust. You're the perfect manager for this abject institution, he muttered. Then, seeing that Miss Pakun had risen and was holding the door open for him, he got up and stalked out, doing his best to slam the outer door of the antechamber behind him. Equipped against such rough treatment, the door merely gave its usual cushioned hiss. Coming at that moment, the sound, which to Mang Huat represented the very soul of luxury, caused him to heave a sigh of pure sensuous pleasure.

That will be all, he told Miss Pakun. She took up her handbag, showed him her most luscious smile for the fraction of a second, and shut the door behind her.

It was now night, and the rain was falling heavily. Miss Pakun would get very wet, he thought, a twinge of pity spicing his satisfaction. He went into the next room and lay back on the divan to watch television for a few minutes. Then he got up. It was the moment to make his evening excursion to the kitchen and, having examined the food, order his dinner. He lighted a cigarette and took the elevator down to the lobby.

In front of the reception desk he frowned with disapproval at the spots left on the carpet by the wet luggage being brought in. At that moment he happened to glance across the crowded lobby, and saw Miss Pakun emerge from the bar, accompanied by the young Englishman. They went directly out into the street. By the time Mang Huat was able to get over to the door, walking at a normal pace, they were climbing into a taxi. He stepped outside, and, sheltered by the marquee, stood watching the cab disappear into the downpour.

On his way to the kitchen he stopped at the cashier's desk, where he recounted to Udom what he had just seen. He also told him to give Miss Pakun her final pay cheque in the morning and to see that under no circumstances was she to get upstairs to his office.

A prostitute, he said with bitter indignation. A common prostitute, masquerading as an intelligent, educated girl.

You Have Left Your Lotus Pods on the Bus

I soon learned not to go near the windows or to draw aside the double curtains in order to look at the river below. The view was wide and lively, with factories and warehouses on the far side of the Chao Phraya, and strings of barges being towed up and down through the dirty water. The new wing of the hotel had been built in the shape of an upright slab, so that the room was high and had no trees to shade it from the poisonous onslaught of the afternoon sun. The end of the day, rather than bringing respite, intensified the heat, for then the entire river was made of sunlight. With the redness of dusk everything out there became melodramatic and forbidding, and still the oven heat from outside leaked through the windows.

Brooks, teaching at Chulalongkorn University, was required as a Fulbright Fellow to attend regular classes in Thai; as an adjunct to this he arranged to spend much of his leisure time with Thais. One day he brought along with him three young men wearing the bright orange-yellow robes of Buddhist monks. They filed into the hotel room in silence and stood in a row as they were presented to me, each one responding by joining his palms together, thumbs touching his chest.

As we talked, Yamyong, the eldest, in his late twenties, explained that he was an ordained monk, while the other two were novices. Brooks then asked Prasert and Vichai if they would be ordained soon, but the monk answered for them.

"I do not think they are expecting to be ordained," he said

quietly, looking at the floor, as if it were a sore subject all too often discussed among them. He glanced up at me and went on talking. "Your room is beautiful. We are not accustomed to such luxury." His voice was flat; he was trying to conceal his disapproval. The three conferred briefly in undertones. "My friends say they have never seen such a luxurious room," he reported, watching me closely through his steel-rimmed spectacles to see my reaction. I failed to hear.

They put down their brown paper parasols and their reticules that bulged with books and fruit. Then they got themselves into position in a row along the couch among the cushions. For a while they were busy adjusting the folds of their robes around their shoulders and legs.

"They make their own clothes," volunteered Brooks. "All the monks do."

I spoke of Ceylon; there the monks bought the robes all cut and ready to sew together. Yamyong smiled appreciatively and said: "We use the same system here."

The air-conditioning roared at one end of the room and the noise of boat motors on the river seeped through the windows at the other. I looked at the three sitting in front of me. They were very calm and self-possessed, but they seemed lacking in physical health. I was aware of the facial bones beneath their skin. Was the impression of sallowness partly due to the shaved eyebrows and hair?

Yamyong was speaking. "We appreciate the opportunity to use English. For this reason we are liking to have foreign friends. English, American; it doesn't matter. We can understand." Prasert and Vichai nodded.

Time went on, and we sat there, extending but not altering the subject of conversation. Occasionally I looked around the room. Before they had come in, it had been only a hotel room whose curtains must be kept drawn. Their presence and their comments on it had managed to invest it with a vaguely disturbing quality; I felt that they considered it a great mistake on my part to have chosen such a place in which to stay.

"Look at his tattoo," said Brooks. "Show him."

Yamyong pulled back his robe a bit from the shoulder, and I saw the two indigo lines of finely written Thai characters. "That is for good health," he said, glancing up at me. His smile seemed odd, but then, his facial expression did not complement his words at any point.

"Don't the Buddhists disapprove of tattooing?" I said.

"Some people say it is backwardness." Again he smiled. "Words for good health are said to be superstition. This was done by my abbot when I was a boy studying in the *wat*. Perhaps he did not know it was a superstition."

We were about to go with them to visit the *wat* where they lived. I pulled a tie from the closet and stood before the mirror arranging it.

"Sir," Yamyong began. "Will you please explain something? What is the significance of the necktie?"

"The significance of the necktie?" I turned to face him. "You mean, why do men wear neckties?"

"No. I know that. The purpose is to look like a gentleman."

I laughed. Yamyong was not put off. "I have noticed that some men wear the two ends equal, and some wear the wide end longer than the narrow, or the narrow longer than the wide. And the neckties themselves, they are not all the same length, are they? Some even with both ends equal reach below the waist. What are the different meanings?"

"There is no meaning," I said. "Absolutely none."

He looked to Brooks for confirmation, but Brooks was trying out his Thai on Prasert and Vichai, and so he was silent and thoughtful for a moment. "I believe you, of course," he said graciously. "But we all thought each way had a different significance attached."

As we went out of the hotel, the doorman bowed respectfully. Until now he had never given a sign that he was aware of my existence. The wearers of the yellow robe carry weight in Thailand.

A few Sundays later I agreed to go with Brooks and our friends to Ayudhaya. The idea of a Sunday outing is so repellent to me that deciding to take part in this one was to a certain extent a compulsive act. Ayudhaya lies less than fifty miles up the Chao Phraya from Bangkok. For historians and art-collectors it is more than just a provincial town; it is a period and a style – having been the Thai capital for more than four centuries. Very likely it still would be, had the Burmese not laid it waste in the eighteenth century.

Brooks came early to fetch me. Downstairs in the street stood the three bhikkus with their book bags and parasols. They hailed a cab, and without any previous price arrangement (the ordinary citizen tries to fix a sum beforehand) we got in and drove for twenty minutes or a half hour, until we got to a bus terminal on the northern outskirts of the city.

It was a nice, old-fashioned, open bus. Every part of it rattled, and the air from the rice fields blew across us as we pieced together our bits of synthetic conversation. Brooks, in high spirits, kept calling across to me: "Look! Water buffaloes!" As we went farther away from Bangkok there were more of the beasts, and his cries became more frequent. Yamyong, sitting next to me, whispered: "Professor Brooks is fond of buffaloes?" I laughed and said I didn't think so.

"Then?"

I said that in America there were no buffaloes in the fields, and that was why Brooks was interested in seeing them. There were no temples in the landscape, either, I told him, and added, perhaps unwisely: "He looks at buffaloes. I look at temples." This struck Yamyong as hilarious, and he made allusions to it now and then all during the day.

The road stretched ahead, straight as a line in geometry, across the verdant, level land. Paralleling it on its eastern side was a fairly wide canal, here and there choked with patches of enormous pink lotuses. In places the flowers were gone and only the pods remained, thick green discs with the circular seeds embedded in their flesh. At the first stop the bhikkus got out. They came aboard again with mangosteens and lotus pods and insisted on giving us large numbers of each. The huge seeds popped out of the fibrous lotus cakes as though from a punchboard; they tasted almost like green almonds. "Something new for you today, I think," Yamyong said with a satisfied air.

Ayudhaya was hot, dusty, spread-out, its surrounding terrain strewn with ruins that scarcely showed through the vegetation. At some distance from the town there began a wide boulevard sparingly lined with important-looking buildings. It continued for a way and then came to an end as abrupt as its beginning. Growing up out of the scrub, and built of small russet-coloured bricks, the ruined temples looked still unfinished rather than damaged by time. Repairs, done in smeared cement, veined their façades.

The bus's last stop was still two or three miles from the centre of Ayudhaya. We got down into the dust, and Brooks declared: "The first thing we must do is find some food. They can't eat anything solid, you know, after midday."

"Not noon exactly," Yamyong said. "Maybe one o'clock or a little later."

"Even so, that doesn't leave much time," I told him. "It's quarter to twelve now."

But the bhikkus were not hungry. None of them had visited Ayudhaya before, and so they compiled a list of things they most wanted to see. They spoke with a man who had a station wagon parked nearby, and we set off for a ruined *stupa* that lay some miles to the southwest. It had been built atop a high mound, which we climbed with some difficulty, so that Brooks could take pictures of us standing within a fissure in the decayed outer wall. The air stank of the bats that lived inside.

When we got back to the bus stop, the subject of food arose once again, but the excursion had put the bhikkus into such a state of excitement that they could not bear to allot time for anything but looking. We went to the museum. It was quiet; there were Khmer heads and documents inscribed in Pali. The day had begun to be painful. I told myself I had known beforehand that it would.

Then we went to a temple. I was impressed, not so much by the gigantic Buddha which all but filled the interior, as by the fact that not far from the entrance a man sat on the floor playing a *ranad* (pronounced *lanat*). Although I was familiar with the sound of it from listening to recordings of Siamese music, I had never before seen the instrument. There was a graduated series of wooden blocks strung together, the whole slung like a hammock over a boat-shaped resonating stand. The tones hurried after one another like drops of water falling very fast. After the painful heat outside, everything in the temple suddenly seemed a symbol of the concept of coolness – the stone floor under my bare feet, the breeze that moved through the shadowy interior, the bamboo fortune sticks being rattled in their long box by those praying at the altar, and the succession of insubstantial, glassy sounds that came from the *ranad*. I thought: If only I could get something to eat, I wouldn't mind the heat so much.

We got into the centre of Ayudhaya a little after three o'clock. It was hot and noisy; the bhikkus had no idea of where to look for a restaurant, and the idea of asking did not appeal to them. The five of us walked aimlessly. I had come to the conclusion that neither Prasert nor Vichai understood spoken English, and I addressed myself earnestly to Yamyong. "*We've got to eat.*" He stared at me with severity. "We are searching," he told me.

Eventually we found a Chinese restaurant on a corner of the principal street. There was a table full of boisterous Thais drinking *mekong* (categorized as whisky, but with the taste of cheap rum) and another table occupied by an entire Chinese family. These people were doing some serious eating, their faces buried in their rice bowls. It cheered me to see them: I was faint, and had half expected to be told that there was no hot food available.

The large menu in English which was brought us must have been typed several decades ago and wiped with a damp rag once a week ever since. Under the heading SPECIALITIES were some dishes that caught my eye, and as I went through the list I began to laugh. Then I read it aloud to Brooks.

Fried Sharks Fins and Bean Sprout
Chicken Chins Stuffed with Shrimp
Fried Rice Birds
Shrimps Balls and Green Marrow
Pigs Lights with Pickles
Braked Rice Bird in Port Wine
Fish Head and Bean Curd

Although it was natural for our friends not to join in the laughter, I felt that their silence was not merely failure to respond; it was heavy, positive.

A moment later three Pepsi-Cola bottles were brought and placed on the table. "What are you going to have?" Brooks asked Yamyong.

"Nothing, thank you," he said lightly. "This will be enough for us today."

"But this is terrible! You mean no one is going to eat *anything?*"

"You and your friend will eat your food," said Yamyong. (He might as well have said "fodder".) Then he, Prasert, and Vichai stood up, and carrying their Pepsi-Cola bottles with them, went to sit at a table on the other side of the room. Now and then Yamyong smiled sternly across at us.

"I wish they'd stop watching us," Brooks said under his breath.

"They were the ones who kept putting it off," I reminded him. But I felt guilty, and I was annoyed at finding myself placed in the position of the self-indulgent unbeliever. It was almost as bad as eating in front of Moslems during Ramadan.

We finished our meal and set out immediately, following Yamyong's decision to visit a certain temple he wanted to see. The taxi drive led us through a region of thorny scrub. Here and there, in the shade of spreading flat-topped trees, were great round pits, full of dark water and crowded with buffaloes; only their wet snouts and horns were visible. Brooks was already crying: "Buffaloes! Hundreds of them!" He asked the taxi driver to stop so that he could photograph the animals.

"You will have buffaloes at the temple," said Yamyong. He was right; there was a muddy pit filled with them only a few hundred feet from the building. Brooks went and took his pictures while the bhikkus paid their routine visit to the shrine. I wandered into a courtyard where there was a long row of stone Buddhas. It is the custom of temple-goers to plaster little squares of gold leaf onto the religious statues in the *wats*. When thousands of them have been stuck onto the same surface, tiny scraps of the gold come unstuck. Then they tremble in the breeze, and the figure shimmers with a small, vibrant life of its own. I stood in the courtyard watching this quivering along the arms and torsos of the Buddhas, and I was reminded of the motion of the bô-tree's leaves. When I mentioned it to Yamyong in the taxi, I think he failed to understand, for he replied: "The bô-tree is a very great tree for Buddhists."

Brooks sat beside me on the bus going back to Bangkok. We spoke only now and then. After so many hours of resisting the heat, it was relaxing to sit and feel the relatively cool air that blew in from the rice fields. The driver of the bus was not a believer in cause and effect. He passed trucks with oncoming traffic in full view. I felt better with my eyes shut, and I might even have dozed off, had there not been in the back of the bus a man, obviously not in control, who was intent on making as much noise as possible. He began to shout, scream, and howl almost as soon as we had left Ayudhaya, and he did this consistently throughout the journey. Brooks and I laughed about it, conjecturing whether he was crazy or only drunk. The aisle was too crowded for me to be able to see him from where I sat. Occasionally I glanced at the other passengers. It was as though they were entirely unaware of the commotion behind them. As we drew closer to the city, the screams became louder and almost constant.

"God, why don't they throw him off?" Brooks was beginning to be annoyed.

"They don't even hear him," I said bitterly. People who can tolerate noise inspire me with envy and rage. Finally I leaned over and said to Yamyong: "That poor man back there! It's incredible!"

"Yes," he said over his shoulder. "He's very busy." This set me thinking what a civilized and tolerant people they were, and I marvelled at the sophistication of the word "busy" to describe what was going on in the back of the bus.

Finally we were in a taxi driving across Bangkok. I would be dropped at my hotel and Brooks would take the three bhikkus on to their *wat*. In my head I was still hearing the heartrending cries. What had the repeated word patterns meant?

I had not been able to give an acceptable answer to Yamyong in his bewilderment about the significance of the necktie, but perhaps he could satisfy my curiosity here.

"That man in the back of the bus, you know?"

Yamyong nodded. "He was working very hard, poor fellow. Sunday is a bad day."

I disregarded the nonsense. "What was he saying?"

"Oh, he was saying: 'Go into second gear,' or 'We are coming to a bridge,' or 'Be careful, people in the road.' Whatever he saw."

Since neither Brooks nor I appeared to have understood, he went on. "All the buses must have a driver's assistant. He watches the road and tells the driver how to drive. It is hard work for him because he must shout loud enough for the driver to hear him."

"But why doesn't he sit up in the front with the driver?"

"No, no. There must be one in the front and one in the back. That way two men are responsible for the bus."

It was an unconvincing explanation for the gruelling sounds we had heard, but to show him that I believed him I said: "Aha! I see."

The taxi drew up in front of the hotel and I got out. When I said good-bye to Yamyong, he replied, I think with a shade of aggrievement: "Good-bye. You have left your lotus pods on the bus."

In the Red Room

When I had a house in Sri Lanka, my parents came out one winter to see me. Originally I had felt some qualms about encouraging their visit. Any one of several things – the constant heat, the unaccustomed food and drinking water, even the presence of a leprosy clinic a quarter of a mile from the house – might easily have an adverse effect on them in one way or another. But I had underestimated their resilience; they made a greater show of adaptability than I had thought possible, and seemed entirely content with everything. They claimed not to mind the lack of running water in the bathrooms, and regularly praised the curries prepared by Appuhamy, the resident cook. Both of them being in their seventies, they were not tempted by the more distant or inaccessible points of interest. It was enough for them to stay around the house reading, sleeping, taking twilight dips in the ocean, and going on short trips along the coast by hired car. If the driver stopped unexpectedly at a shrine to sacrifice a coconut, they were delighted, and if they came upon a group of elephants lumbering along the road, the car had to be parked some distance up ahead, so that they could watch them approach and file past. They had no interest in taking photographs, and this spared me what is perhaps the most taxing duty of a cicerone: the repeated waits while the ritual between man and machine is observed. They were ideal guests.

Colombo, where all the people I knew lived, was less than a hundred miles away. Several times we went up for weekends, which I arranged with friends by telephone beforehand. There we had tea on the wide verandas of certain houses in Cinnamon Gardens, and sat at dinners with professors from the university, Protestant ministers, and assorted members of the government. (Many of the Sinhalese found it strange that I should call my parents by their first names, Dodd and Hannah; several of them inquired if I were actually their son or had been adopted.) These weekends in the city were hot and exhausting, and they were always happy to get back to the house, where they could change into comfortable clothing.

One Sunday not long before they were due to return to America, we decided to take in the horse races at Gintota, where there are also some botanical gardens that Hannah wanted to see. I engaged rooms at the New Oriental in Galle and we had lunch there before setting out.

As usual, the events were late in starting. It was the spectators, in any case, who were the focus of interest. The phalanx of women in their shot-silk saris moved Hannah to cries of delight. The races themselves were something of a disappointment. As we left the grounds, Dodd said with satisfaction: It'll be good to get back to the hotel and relax.

But we were going to the Botanical Gardens, Hannah reminded him. I'd like to have just a peek at them.

Dodd was not eager. Those places cover a lot of territory, you know, he said.

We'll just look inside and come out again, she promised.

The hired car took us to the entrance. Dodd was tired, and as a result was having a certain amount of difficulty in walking. The last year or so I find my legs aren't always doing exactly what I want 'em to do, he explained.

You two amble along, Hannah told us. I'll run up ahead and find if there's anything to see.

We stopped to look up at a clove tree; its powerful odour filled the air like a gas. When we turned to continue our walk, Hannah was no longer in sight. We went on under the high vegetation, around a curve in the path, looked ahead, and still there was no sign of her.

What does your mother think she's doing? The first thing we know she'll be lost.

She's up ahead somewhere.

Soon, at the end of a short lane overhung by twisted lianas, we saw her, partially hidden by the gesticulating finger of a Sinhalese standing next to her.

What's going on? Dodd hastened his steps. Run over there, he told me, and I started ahead, walking fast. Then I saw Hannah's animated smile, and slowed my pace. She and the young man stood in front of a huge bank of brown spider orchids.

Ah! I thought we'd lost you, I said.

Look at these orchids. Aren't they incredible?

Dodd came up, nodded at the young man, and examined the display of flowers. They look to me like skunk cabbage, he declared.

The young man broke into wild laughter. Dodd stared at him.

This young man has been telling me the history of the garden, Hannah began hurriedly. About the opposition to it, and how it finally came to be planted. It's interesting.

The Sinhalese beamed triumphantly. He wore white flannels and a crimson blazer, and his sleek black hair gave off a metallic blue glint in the sunlight.

Ordinarily I steer a determined course away from the anonymous person who tries to engage me in conversation. This time it was too late; encouraged by Hannah, the stranger strolled beside her, back to the main path. Dodd and I exchanged a glance, shrugged, and began to follow along behind.

Somewhere up at the end of the gardens a pavilion had been built under the high rain-trees. It had a veranda where a few sarong-draped men reclined in long chairs. The young man stopped walking. Now I invite you to a cold ginger beer.

Oh, Hannah said, at a loss. Well, yes. That would be nice. I'd welcome a chance to sit down.

Dodd peered at his wristwatch. I'll pass up the beer, but I'll sit and watch you.

We sat and looked out at the lush greenness. The young man's conversation leapt from one subject to another; he seemed unable to follow any train of thought farther than its inception. I put this down as a bad sign, and tried to tell from the inflections of Hannah's voice whether she found him as disconcerting as I did.

Dodd was not listening. He found the heat of low-country Ceylon oppressive, and it was easy to see that he was tired. Thinking I might cover up the young man's chatter, I turned to Dodd and began to talk about whatever came into my head: the resurgence of mask-making in Ambalangoda, devil-dancing, the high incidence of crime among the fishermen converted to Catholicism. Dodd listened, but did no more than move his head now and then in response.

Suddenly I heard the young man saying to Hannah: I have just the house for you. A godsend to fill your requirements. Very quiet and protected.

She laughed. Mercy, no! We're not looking for a house. We're only going to be here a few weeks more.

I looked hard at her, hoping she would take my glance as a warning against going on and mentioning the place where she was staying. The young man was not paying attention, in any case. Quite all right. You are not buying houses. But you should see this house and tell your friends. A superior investment, no doubt about that. Shall I introduce myself, please? Justus Gonzag, called Sonny by friends.

His smile, which was not a smile at all, gave me an unpleasant physical sensation.

Come anyway. A five-minute walk, guaranteed. He looked searchingly at Hannah. I intend to give you a book of poems. My own. Autographed for you with your name. That will make me very happy.

Oh, Hannah said, a note of dismay in her voice. Then she braced herself and smiled. That would be lovely. But you understand, we can't stay more than a minute.

There was a silence. Dodd inquired plaintively: Can't we go in the car, at least?

Impossible, sir. We are having a very narrow road. Car can't get through. I am arranging in a jiffy. He called out. A waiter came up, and he addressed him in Sinhalese at some length. The man nodded and went inside. Your driver is now bringing your car to this gate. Very close by.

This was going a little too far. I asked him how he thought anyone was going to know which car was ours.

No problem. I was present when you were leaving the Pontiac. Your driver is called Wickramasinghe. Up-country resident, most reliable. Down here people are hopeless.

I disliked him more each time he spoke. You're not from around here? I asked him.

No, no! I'm a Colombo chap. These people are impossible scoundrels. Every one of the blighters has a knife in his belt, guaranteed.

When the waiter brought the check, he signed it with a rapid flourish and stood up. Shall we be going on to the house, then?

No one answered, but all three of us rose and reluctantly moved off with him in the direction of the exit gate. The hired car was there; Mr Wickramasinghe saluted us from behind the wheel.

The afternoon heat had gone, leaving only a pocket here and there beneath the trees where the air was still. Originally the lane where we were walking had been wide enough to admit a bullock-cart, but the vegetation encroaching on each side had narrowed it to little more than a footpath.

At the end of the lane were two concrete gateposts with no gate between them. We passed through, and went into a large compound bordered on two sides by ruined stables. With the exception of one small ell, the house was entirely hidden by high bushes and flowering trees. As we came to a doorway the young man stopped and turned to us, holding up one finger. No noises here, isn't it? Only birds.

It was the hour when the birds begin to awaken from their daytime lethargy. An indeterminate twittering came from the trees. He lowered his finger and turned back to the door. Mornings they are singing. Now not.

Oh, it's lovely, Hannah told him.

He led us through a series of dark empty rooms. Here the dhobi was washing the soiled clothing. This is the kitchen, you see? Ceylon style. Only the charcoal. My father was refusing paraffin and gas both. Even in Colombo.

We huddled in a short corridor while he opened a door, reached in, and flooded the space inside with blinding light. It was a small room, made to seem still smaller by having been given glistening crimson walls and ceiling. Almost all the space was filled by a big bed with a satin coverlet of a slightly darker red. A row of straight-backed chairs stood along one wall. Sit down and be comfy, our host advised us.

We sat, staring at the bed and at the three framed pictures on the wall above its brass-spoked headboard: on the left a girl, in the middle our host, and on the right another young man. The portraits had the imprecision of passport photographs that have been enlarged many times their original size.

Hannah coughed. She had nothing to say. The room gave off a cloying scent of ancient incense, as in a disused chapel. The feeling of absurdity I got from seeing us sitting there side by side, wedged in between the bed and the wall, was so powerful that it briefly paralysed my mental processes. For once the young man was being silent; he sat stiffly, looking straight ahead, like someone at the theatre.

Finally I had to say something. I turned to our host and asked him if he slept in this room. The question seemed to shock him. Here? he cried, as if the thing were inconceivable. No, no! This house is unoccupied. No one sleeping on the premises. Only a stout chap to watch out at night. Excuse me one moment.

He jumped up and hurried out of the room. We heard his footsteps echo in the corridor and then grow silent. From somewhere in the house there came the sonorous chiming of a grandfather clock; its comfortable sound made the shiny blood-coloured cubicle even more remote and unlikely.

Dodd stirred uncomfortably in his chair; the bed was too close for him to cross his legs. As soon as he comes back, we go, he muttered.

He's looking for the book, I imagine, said Hannah.

We waited a while. Then I said: Look. If he's not back in two minutes, I move we just get up and leave. We can find our way out all right.

Hannah objected, saying it would be unpardonable.

Again we sat in silence. Dodd was now shielding his eyes from the glare. When Sonny Gonzag returned, he was carrying a glass of water which he drank standing in the doorway. His expression had altered: he now looked preoccupied, and he was breathing heavily.

We slowly got to our feet, Hannah still looking expectant.

We are going, then? Come. With the empty glass still in his hand he turned off the lights, shut the door behind us, opened another, and led us quickly through a sumptuous room furnished with large divans, Coromandel screens and bronze Buddhas. We had no time to do more than glance from side to side as we followed him. As we went out through the front door, he called one peremptory word back into the house, presumably to the caretaker.

There was a wide unkempt lawn on this side, where a few clumps of high areca palms were being slowly strangled by the sheaths of philodendron roots and leaves that encased their trunks. Creepers had spread themselves unpleasantly over the tops of shrubs like the meshes of gigantic cobwebs. I knew that Hannah was thinking of snakes. She kept her eyes on the ground, stepping carefully from flagstone to flagstone as we followed the exterior of the house around to the stables, and thence out into the lane.

The swift twilight had come down. No one seemed disposed to speak. When we reached the car Mr Wickramasinghe stood beside it.

Cheery-bye, then, and tell your friends to look for Sonny Gonzag when they are coming to Gintota. He offered his hand to Dodd first, then me, finally to Hannah, and turned away.

They were both very quiet on the way back to Galle. The road was narrow and the blinding lights of oncoming cars made them nervous. During dinner we made no mention of the afternoon.

At breakfast, on the veranda swept by the morning breeze, we felt sufficiently removed from the experience to discuss it. Hannah said: I kept waking up in the night and seeing that awful bed.

Dodd groaned.

I said it was like watching television without the sound. You saw everything, but you didn't get what was going on.

The kid was completely non compos mentis. You could see that a mile away, Dodd declared.

Hannah was not listening. It must have been a maid's room. But why would he take us there? I don't know; there's something terribly depressing about the whole thing. It makes me feel a little sick just to think about it. And that bed!

Well, stop thinking about it, then! Dodd told her. I for one am going to put it right out of my mind. He waited. I feel better already. Isn't that the way the Buddhists do it?

The sunny holiday continued for a few weeks more, with longer trips now to the east, to Tissamaharana and the wild elephants in the Yala Preserve. We did not go to Colombo again until it was time for me to put them onto the plane.

The black weather of the monsoons was blowing in from the southwest as we drove up the coast. There was a violent downpour when we arrived in mid-afternoon at Mount Lavinia and checked into our rooms. The crashing of the waves outside my room was so loud that Dodd had to shut the windows in order to hear what we were saying.

I had taken advantage of the trip to Colombo to arrange a talk with my lawyer, a Telugu-speaking Indian. We were to meet in the bar at the Galleface, some miles up the coast. I'll be back at six, I told Hannah. The rain had abated somewhat when I started out.

Damp winds moved through the lobby of the Galleface, but the smoky air in the bar was stirred only by fans. As I entered, the first person I noticed was Weston of the Chartered Bank. The lawyer had not yet come in, so I stood at the bar with Weston and ordered a whisky.

Didn't I see you in Gintota at the races last month? With an elderly couple?

I was there with my parents. I didn't notice you.

I couldn't tell. It was too far away. But I saw the same three people later with a local character. What did you think of Sonny Gonzag?

I laughed. He dragged us off to his house.

You know the story, I take it.

I shook my head.

The story, which he recounted with relish, began on the day after Gonzag's wedding, when he stepped into a servant's room and found his bride in bed with the friend who had been best man. How he happened to have a pistol with him was not explained, but he shot them both in the face, and later chopped their bodies into pieces. As Weston remarked: That sort of thing isn't too uncommon, of course. But it was the trial that caused the scandal. Gonzag spent a few weeks in a mental hospital, and was discharged.

You can imagine, said Weston. Political excitement. The poor go to jail for a handful of rice, but the rich can kill with impunity, and that sort of thing. You still see references to the case in the press now and then.

I was thinking of the crimson blazer and the Botanical Gardens. No. I never heard about it, I said.

He's mad as a hatter, but there he is, free to do whatever he feels like. And all he wants now is to get people into that house and show them the room where the great event took place. The more the merrier as far as he's concerned.

I saw the Indian come into the bar. It's unbelievable, but I believe it, I told Weston.

Then I turned to greet the lawyer, who immediately complained of the stale air in the bar. We sat and talked in the lounge.

I managed to get back to Mount Lavinia in time to bathe

before dinner. As I lay in the tepid water, I tried to imagine the reactions of Hannah and Dodd when I told them what I had heard. I myself felt a solid satisfaction at knowing the rest of the story. But being old, they might well brood over it, working it up into an episode so unpleasant in retrospect that it stained the memory of their holiday. I still had not decided whether to tell them or not when I went to their room to take them down to dinner.

We sat as far away from the music as we could get. Hannah had dressed a little more elaborately than usual, and they were both speaking with more than their accustomed animation. I realized that they were happy to be returning to New York. Halfway through the meal they began to review what they considered the highlights of their visit. They mentioned the Temple of the Tooth, the pair of Bengal tiger cubs in Dehiwala which they had petted but regretfully declined to purchase, the Indonesian dinner on Mr Bultjens's lawn, where the myna bird had hopped over to Hannah and said: "Eat it up", the cobra under the couch at Mrs de Sylva's tea party.

And that peculiar young man in the *strange* house, Hannah added meditatively.

Which one was that? asked Dodd, frowning as he tried to remember. Then it came to him. Oh, God, he muttered. Your special friend. He turned to me. Your mother certainly can pick 'em.

Outside, the ocean roared. Hannah seemed lost in thought. *I* know what it was like! she exclaimed suddenly. It was like being shown around one of the temples by a bhikku. Isn't that what they call them?

Dodd sniffed. Some temple! he chuckled.

No, I'm serious. That room had a particular meaning for him. It was like a sort of shrine.

I looked at her. She had got to the core without needing the details. I felt that, too, I said. Of course, there's no way of knowing.

She smiled. Well, what you don't know won't hurt you.

I had heard her use the expression a hundred times without ever being able to understand what she meant by it, because it seemed so patently untrue. But for once it was apt. I nodded my head and said: That's right.

Glossary

adoul (singular: adel)   notaries
Aid el Kebir   the annual Sacrifice of the Sheep
aoulidi   my son
arroyo   a rivulet
baraka   beneficent psychic power (by extension, an amulet providing protection)
barranca   a ravine
benadir (singular: bendir)   disc-shaped drums
bhikku   a Buddhist monk
Bismil'lah   In the name of Allah
cabrozels   crescent-shaped tarts filled with almond paste
chedis   spires topping the larger Buddhist temples
comedor   dining-room
dillal   auctioneer
fondouq   caravanserai
fqih   a man supposedly versed in the Koran, often consulted as exorcist
gandoura   a loose-fitting sleeveless male garment
haïk   the traditional female outer garment
Hamdoul'lah   Thanks to Allah
Jilala   a religious brotherhood
joteya   flea-market
majoun   jam, made of fruit, honey and nuts, often containing cannabis
mejdoub   a madman who is also a Cherif and thus cannot be considered mad
mijmah   a brazier
moqqaddem   the leader of a group of musicians performing the ritual music of a religious brotherhood
mrozeiya   a festive dish in which meat is cooked in honey

189

msid   a Koranic primary school
ni hablar   out of the question
oued   river or dry riverbed
pinchitos   meat broiled on skewers
qachla   barracks
qadi   a judge
qahouaji   man who prepares tea or serves it in a café
qoubba   a sanctuary, often the tomb of a local saint
riad   an enclosed garden
sebsi   kif pipe
selham   a hooded cape (same as burnous)
smayyim   the hottest period of summer
stupa   a monument, often built to house sacred relics
taifor   a low round table
tajine   a stew
tchar   a village
tolba (singular: taleb)   divinity students
wat   Buddhist temple
zigdoun   woman's indoor garment